The *Will* to Kill

A Murder Mystery

by Marianne Flatley Correri

Copyright © Marianne Flatley Correri

Prelude

It was a most frightening feeling, and one she never experienced before this terrifying moment. The smallest piece of bagel got lodged in her windpipe, and wouldn't budge. At one point she tried to clear her throat as she placed a fist under her sternum to push the darned thing up. Her body told her to stand, that it was imperative that she rise from her chair. And in that second, just before the morsel decided to move along to where it belonged, she feared that, had she choked and died that instant, that nobody would be there to take care of Pa. She was all he had. And coming that close to death at the age of thirty-two told Kara Fitzgerald that nobody was immune from it. Nobody. Even the strange little blue bird that perched outside the kitchen window and was, literally, looking straight at her. Was he trying to tell her something? That life was precious, and fleeting?

She had cheated it, death, in that moment. Pure and simple. Others, however, would not be as fortunate. Somewhere, at that very moment, someone was dying. In fact, the very next day, some executives from the North Jersey Bank were about to be reminded of the inevitable for all of us. Reminded in a way that none of them would ever forget.

****

It began as one of the five best days of the year. Weather-wise. A lovely day. More lovely because the annual executive meeting was away from the stuffy office. For the next thirty-six hours, everyone would be treated to fresh, clean mountain air. First on the agenda was a three mile hike around the old Hague mansion. A tranquil, woodsy setting, it was the perfect place to enjoy the beauty of nature, away from annoying conference calls and disgruntled clients. Peace. Quiet. Life.

"Watch for stray rocks," the energetic young hiking guide instructed. "And, in the unlikely event we encounter a bear," he paused for the usual nervous laughter, "stay calm, quiet and let them pass." Then someone called out "THEM?!" which evoked more nervous laughter. "Yes. It's not uncommon to see a mother and her cubs. They won't bother you if you don't bother them."

But none of his warnings could prepare the group for what they were about to stumble upon. A body. The body of a man. But not an ordinary man. Sticking out of the man's sweatshirt was a Roman collar attached to a black shirt. This man was a priest..

Chapter One

Kara Fitzgerald's "bagel scare," as it came to be known in her recollections, was a sign that there were no guarantees in life, and that she had to take action regarding her Pa. If something were to happen to her, he'd be utterly alone. But the right thing to do wasn't always the easy thing, or the comfortable thing. She was already displaying signs of trepidation as she ran her thumb and index finger through the same strand of long blonde hair. Over and over again. It was a nervous habit she picked up back in grade school whenever a math or science test loomed large. Now, at thirty-two, with math and science, thankfully, in life's rearview mirror, Kara's nerves were acting up for another reason. This time it was because she knew she had no choice. It was time. Time to put her beloved Pa in what was once called "a home."

But as much as she knew she had no choice, she still felt wretched. Kara had made a promise to her mother two years ago as Ann Fitzgerald lay on her death bed, etched with pain and riddled with cancer, that she'd keep Pa in their house, no matter how bad the dementia got. Now she had to go back on that promise. And breaking a promise, especially to her dead mother, sucked. It was out of character for Kara to go back on her word, especially to the loving couple who adopted her as an infant thirty-two years ago and treated her, every moment, as if she were the most precious thing in the world. And to them, she was.

Desmond and Ann Fitzgerald brought the tiny tow-headed baby girl home on a warm April day. Kara couldn't imagine growing up with a better life. If the adage is true, that we pick our parents, that before we take human form, we search the earth for the people who will provide what we need as we navigate our way through the start of life, then Kata hit the jackpot. Not monetarily, as money in the Fitzgerald home was always tight, but in terms of love, kindness, generosity. The important things in life.

Still, for the Fitzgerald's to have her as their child, it meant somebody else didn't want her. And Kara could only presume that God knew what He was doing and that her adoption was meant to be; that "God picked you out just for us" as her mother used to say. In fact, she heard that so often that Kara never was prompted to look for her birth parents the way other adopted children often did. For Kara, there was no need.

Life growing up was very good. Kara was on her way to success, working after graduation from Montclair State as a reporter on the local crime beat for the North Jersey *Beacon*. Dating here and there. Saving money to eventually move out and get her own place. Then, when her mother got sick, Kara put her personal plans on hold. After Ann died, Pa's dementia got worse. Kara gave up her dream job at the *Beacon* to care for him. She did it out of love, and a promise she made to her dying mother … that she would always keep Pa at home.

Still, it was a challenging and bone tiring job for one person. Even a young person. But Kara wouldn't have it any other way. Until now. Especially lately, as her hand was being forced by Pa's nocturnal wanderings and dangerous behaviors.

On a recent afternoon, after returning from the grocery store, Kara found an empty pot on a lit burner. Then Pa started to have accidents. Often. But pulling the plug on the electric stove or buying Depends were only temporary fixes. Soon he began to wander around after dark, no matter how many locks and bolts Kara put on the doors. Twice in one week, while Kara slept, Pa shuffled into the night and took a stroll around the neighborhood. If it weren't for the off-duty cop coming home from his shift who spotted Pa in his underwear in forty degrees, temperatures,

Pa might have ended up a popsicle in the morgue. Kara hoped it was a one-off, but a few nights after that Pa left home again and wound up outside a widowed neighbor's bedroom window, banging and demanding to be let in. No charges were pressed, thank goodness. But what was to prevent it from happening again ... with a neighbor who wasn't as forgiving.

With fewer and fewer bullets left to dodge, Kara knew that the only answer was to put Pa into Twin Oaks, the assisted living center nearby. But Twin Oaks was pricey, and to afford it, Pa would need to turn over all of his social security checks to pay for his care, and Kara would need to sell the house to pay the balance. Then, once the house sold, she'd need to find her own place to live, and a job to pay the rent on that new place.

Kara took a sip of tea then glanced over at the wonderful man who taught her how to be kind. He was in his own world, happily watching reruns that were older than Kara. It was the same episode of "Gunsmoke," followed by "Judge Judy." He'd already seen them a dozen times, but for Pa they were the first time as the dementia played tricks on his mind. Everything old was new again.

As she watched him enjoying the programs from his ratty old wing chair, Kara studied the frail little man who once had arms like Popeye. Pa's days as a robust foreman on a construction crew were long gone, just like his muscles and his once dark auburn hair. Now he was a half of his old self, half man, half child. His innocent expression, which he adopted recently, was full of wonder. So trusting. And it was the guilt of having to uproot this sweet, trusting man, to leave him in a new place, that made Kara feel wretched. She was about to betray the loving father who never, ever betrayed her.

"What did you say, darlin'?" He turned to her and smiled.

"I guess I was talking to myself."

"Hear anything interestin'?" he laughed. Pa was full of corny comebacks, and Kara knew every one of them. She laughed, the way people do when they're trying to sound like it was the first time they were exposed to such hilarity.

"You're funny, Pa," But her response fell on deaf ears. The expression of fun on Pa's face suddenly vanished, replaced by a look of confusion, and sadness. This was his "new" self, a personality that was making its appearance with more and more regularity.

It hurt Kara to see her beloved father slipping away. But she could do nothing else but soldier on. She was the grown-up now. And as the adult in the room, she had to make the painful decisions. That decision was today. Today was the day Pa would be a new guest at Twin Oaks. Mrs. Warren, the director, was expecting them. They'd arrive in time for lunch.

"C'mon, Pa. We have to leave now for our lunch." But Pa's eyes were glued on the TV. "Pa? Did you hear me? We've got to go ... to our lunch."

"But .. but it's Judge Judy."

"Judge Judy is over, Pa." The opening theme for *Matlock* came on the screen. "Pa?"

"I want to watch Ben," he said defiantly, his eyes centered on Andy Griffith playing the crime-solving Atlanta barrister.

. "Pa, we have to leave now. For our lunch. Or there will be no food left."

"Lunch?" He considered it. Then, "I'll eat here." She knew if she didn't get him out of the house now, she'd have a devil of a time doing so later. Pa was rigid about staying faithful to his Triple Crown of murder mysteries Matlock, Murder She Wrote and the original Perry

Mason's.

"It's a rerun, Pa. You already know how it's gonna turn out. Let's go get a delicious

lunch. I've found a new place I think you'll like."

"This is NOT a rerun, Kara!" he banged a foot. Then, softening in the next moment, .

"Where are we going?"

Kara saw the opening she needed and took it. "To a nice place. With nice people. I hear

the food they serve is delicious."

He looked down at himself as if wondering how he magically transformed out of his

customary uniform of sweatshirt and baggy pants into a smart pair of khaki slacks and a plaid

shirt. Kara chose the simple ensemble as it was Pa's favorite going-out outfit. The same

combination he always wore whenever he and her mother went to dinner on Saturday nights.

Back in the day. When they were both themselves.

"Did I put these on? I don't like this shirt."

"You look very handsome. Like you stepped right out of the Sears catalog." she added. It

was Pa's favorite expression whenever he thought someone looked good. Though Kara had

never seen a Sears catalog and presumed it was a compliment, of sorts.

"I do?"

"Let me help you up," she positioned herself along the side of Pa's chair, placing her

hand under his elbow.

"No, I need no help," he shooed her away, then slowly rose to his feet. Kara drew in a long breath. Now it would be another five or so minutes while he shuffled to the front door. She could only pray he wouldn't stop along the way to ask more questions. He was full of them. And they were always the same.

"Where are we going?"

"To have lunch."

He shuffled some more. Kara drew in another breath, a prayer for patience. Only this time she forgot to exhale. It stuck in her diaphragm as she watched the man she adored slowly, methodically, painstakingly make his way across the worn carpet toward the front door.

As she tried to guide his steps without appearing to be guiding his steps, Kara's eyes fell on a patchy spot in the avocado wall-to-wall and wondered if there were hardwoods underneath. It was the kind of random thing that popped into her head from time to time as she waited for Pa to finish eating, or to shuffle to his chair, or to go to the bathroom or get into bed. A slow parade of time, time that not only belonged to Pa but also to her. Time that was just passing them by. But while Pa's time was just that ...passing. Kara's was her future. The future that was on hold ... for the time being.

It was a conundrum. On one hand, Kara wanted Pa around. On the other hand, she knew things couldn't go on this way. It wasn't safe, for one thing. And it wasn't fair. Not fair to Pa because he was locked away all day with only the company of the TV and TV make believe. At Twin Oaks, he'd hopefully make friends his own age. And it wasn't fair, and this was the part that made Kara feel guilty, to her. But was it so wrong to want to live her own life? To go back to a job and to be around people her own age. It had now been nearly three years since she'd been waiting ... waiting for Mom to get well, and then waiting when that didn't happen for her to die. Waiting for Pa to get along without his spouse, then watching him slide into the quicksand of dementia. Three whole years she'd already spent as a prisoner of love. A prisoner of self-imposed loneliness too. While other young women her age were marrying and starting families, or moving up in their careers, she was on hold ... waiting ... and feeling like the world was passing her by.

"That's it, Pa. One foot in front of the other. We're nearly at the door."

"Where are we going?"

"To have a nice lunch. And meet some nice people." Kara tried to sound as if she was hearing Pa's questions for the first time. It wasn't his fault that his mind made him repeat ... and repeat.

He was in her care ... a helpless child in many ways, and a far cry from the man who could build anything, crack jokes at the drop of a hat, and loved his wife and daughter deeply. Desmond Fitzgerald was once a man's man with a huge heart. He was kind and respectful to everyone, and never hesitated to do a favor for a friend ... or anyone in need if he could.

If a neighbor's car battery went dead, Des was there with jumper cables, even on the coldest winter day. If he got word that a local family was down on their luck, Des would quietly drop off a bag of groceries on their doorstep. He did home repair projects for elderly widows in town and refused to accept a dime. That was her Pa, the man Kara chose to remember.

"Where are we going?" They were nearing the front door.

"When we step onto the landing, Pa, you grab the railing, okay?"

His blue eyes met hers and he smiled. "You're a good girl." Then he added with a devilish twinkle, "I don't care what they say!"

"Oh, Pa. I love you!."

"I love you too, Darlin'."

They inched their way down the steps, slowly, until they finally reached the front walk. Suddenly Pa stopped. His placid expression turned angry. Narrowed eyes. A scowl. "What the hell is that?!" Kara turned to where he was staring and saw the "For Sale" sign. "Who put *that* there?!. *I'm* not selling our house!"

"Must be a mistake, Pa." She hated lying. "I'll take care of it."

"Some mistake! Who do they think they are?!" His anger was ratcheting up. Fast.

"It's okay. I'll get rid of the sign." She made sure his hands were on the bottom of the railing then she rushed over to the sign and yanked it dramatically out of the ground, tossing it into the bushes. She'd replace it later. "There. It's gone. Now let's get in the car and go to our lunch."

She opened the passenger's side to help him into her Civic. Then she moved to the driver's side. No sooner had she opened her door when a sparkling white Lexus blocked the driveway. She knew who it was. Connie Belford. The realtor. The same Connie whose face was plastered all over town on every sign, billboard, shopping cart and community trash can she could find. But this Connie wasn't "photoshopped" Connie. The Connie whose Crayola yellow hair was artfully blow-dried toward heaven, whose skin was ironed and starched till it was wrinkle-free. This Connie was not the Connie in those photos who looked ten years younger and ten pounds lighter. No, the woman clomping across the front lawn was the *real* Connie. The Connie who wore heavy cologne, orange lipstick and had a face that could catch a three day rain. But ... and this was the important part about Connie Belford ... she could sell houses! Fast. And that's what Kara needed if she was going to have enough money in sixty days to pay the balance to Twin Oaks.

"Oh, Kaaa-ra! Kaaa-ra!" she called as she beckoned to the embarrassed young Asian couple trailing behind her. Kara felt sorry for them immediately. She herself could only take a few minutes of Connie. These poor people were trapped in the car with her all day.

"Who is that *nut*?" Pa barked.

"I'll be right back." She got out of the car and cut Connie off at the pass. "Now's not a good time," Kara said softly.

Connie maintained her outdoor voice. "You mean he doesn't know you're selling?!"

"I can't talk now. We have an appointment at Twin Oaks. Please move your car." Kara returned to her car and began to slowly inch backwards. But Connie wasn't finished. She walked around to Pa's side, bent down so her face was nearly touching the window, and called out loudly, "Good luck, Mister Fitzgerald!"

"What the hell is she talking about?!" Pa quipped.

Kara changed the subject. "I hear the chef at Twin Oaks is very good." Pa didn't answer. Instead, he stared ahead. Still fuming. But Kara wasn't sure about what. It could be the "for sale" sign or it could be Connie Belford blocking the driveway or something entirely different. That was how dementia worked. But on the plus side, Kara knew Pa's bad humor would change soon. That was the thing about dementia. People forgot what they were mad about.

She checked her rearview mirror. Connie had moved her Lexus. Kara backed out as quickly as she could, hoping Pa wouldn't notice that Connie and the Asian couple were now heading across the front lawn, on their way to the house.

She held her breath. If Pa saw them entering his home, Kara knew she'd have to stop the car. He would demand, take a fit, want to see what was going on. Then it would take forever to get him back into the car ... if at all.

"Pa, don't you think it's a beautiful day? I love the fall." Her tone was intentionally calm as she pointed to a maple tree across the street. Thankfully, Pa took the bait and turned to look at the tree. Kara exhaled.

They drove in an uncomfortable silence Kara tried to make conversation but Pa was biting his lips, a sign that he was still angry ... and confused. Then the Civic merged onto the highway. They were passing a large cemetery ... not the one where her mother was buried. Kara used the moment to her advantage. She set her father up to make another one of his corny jokes.

"That's a big cemetery, isn't it, Pa?" Then she waited. Soon a curve came over his lips. He's taken the bait.

"Darlin,' you know how many people are dead in that cemetery?" Kara smiled. She'd heard this one, like all the others, thousands of times before. Now it was her turn to play the sucker.

"No, Pa, how many?"

"All of them!" Then he broke into uproarious laughter and she joined in.

"Hey, Pa. That's a good one!" If she could slap her knee to add more animation to her reaction, she would have. But her mission had been successful. Pa had forgotten about the For Sale sign on the front lawn. He forgot about missing Matlock and Perry and now all that was left for Kara was the last hurdle. Getting her dear, trusting, confused father to enter and to *stay* at Twin Oaks.

They turned off the highway onto a long, tree lined road that led to the entrance of the upscale assisted living center. Yesterday, when Kara came to sign the papers, leaving Pa in the care of her kind next door neighbor while he watched *Wheel of Fortune,* she was pleasantly surprised at how clean and happy and peaceful the place seemed to be. The staff was cordial and welcoming. Most of the "guests" as they were called, were about Pa's age. And when she drove away from the place, seeing the October leaves falling quietly onto the lush green landscape, she felt good about her decision.

Now, as the Civic weaved its way around curves in the oak-lined road, past huge splashing fountains and teakwood benches occupied by wily squirrels or chirping sparrows, Kara glanced over to see Pa's reaction. His face was lifted. His mouth held the glint of a smile. She was happy to see that he was feeling the glorious peace that surrounded this place ... until ...

The Civic turned down the road leading to the main building. The majestic mansion stretched out before them, but blocking it was ... chaos. Like a splash of ice water on a frigid day, they were hit with the view of vans and trucks and antennae and people with microphones in the distance. Reporters. Preening before cameras. A mess of media pests. As peaceful as yesterday had been when Kara came here, today was the exact opposite, as if a horde of human locusts descended and took up residence right in front of the main entrance to Twin Oaks. Reporters blocked the path to the front parking lot, making access to the entrance impossible.

"Food here must be darned good to get this kinda crowd," Pa said in earnest, nonplussed by the nonsense. He had no idea, Kara thought, what was going on. And in truth, neither did she.

She inched the car through the throng. The reporter in her wondered what happened to warrant such a big story ... and judging by the amount of media coverage, it *was* a big news story.

"Where can I park?" Kara thought aloud. Then she spotted an impeccably groomed, middle-aged man in a black livery. He was waving her down, as if he'd been waiting for her and Pa to arrive. Kara followed his directions and found a parking spot around the back, near an employees' entrance. The man met her at the car. He had a friendly smile that lit up his large face.

"I'm Daniel, Miss Fitzgerald. I believe we were introduced yesterday."

"Yes. I remember. Hello, Daniel." She nodded toward the chaos. "What's going on?"

"Sadly we lost one of our guests last night." Daniel was cautious about his choice of words.

"Lost someone?!" Pa blurted out. "Did you check the restroom?"

Daniel looked past Kara, smiled, and addressed Pa. "Nice to meet you Des. I'm Daniel. Welcome to Twin Oaks."

"Did they leave without paying the check? I mean the one you lost." Pa was deadly serious. Daniel held back a chuckle. Kara could tell he was used to this kind of thing. She liked him already.

"Hey, Des, today we've got shrimp cocktail on the menu ... and filet mignon. Apple pie for dessert. Sound good to you?" Pa nodded and smiled. "I thought so." Daniel moved around to Pa's side of the car. Kara could see he had brought a wheelchair ... a very elegant, sleek, "Rolls Royce" of wheelchairs. "Des, I brought my chariot. Just for you!" Daniel was already helping Pa out of the car. He made it all look so easy. "Goes from zero to sixty in two seconds flat. Whadda ya say we take 'er for a spin?" Kara waited to see Pa's reaction. He wasn't the kind of guy to easily accept a ride in a wheelchair. But he didn't seem to mind as Daniel helped him into the seat. "There we are! Now ... how about we make a beeline for the dining room? I can smell that filet mignon from here!"

Pa was going along. Kara was holding her breath. Another hurdle was over. But did Pa know, deep down, that they weren't here for the filet mignon? Kara sensed that he did, but he was being a good sport about it ... at least for now.

They arrived at a side entrance. Kara was grateful that none of the reporters in front knew about this door or she'd never be able to get Pa inside quite as smoothly.

She rushed to keep up with Daniel, who was already ferrying her father down a long, carpeted corridor. An elixir of luscious aromas awaited in the distance. Daniel was right. She could smell steaks on the grill. And garlic. And was that fresh baked bread? She wished, at least for a moment, that she could sign herself up as a "guest.". But only for a moment.

By the time Kara caught up with Daniel and Pa, they were already getting settled at a table of other men. Daniel helped Pa into a dining room chair, then bent down to remind him that "I'm your go-to guy. Anything you need, Des, I'm here to take care of it." Pa nodded the way little children nod while listening to their favorite teacher. "And it's okay if I call you Des?" Uh-oh, Kara thought. Daniel didn't yet realize it but he was setting himself up for one of Pa's corny quips. She could tell by the wry smile that came over her father's face. "Sure! You can call me Des," Pa paused. "Just never call me late for supper!" Then Pa broke into rip-roaring laughter. Daniel went along, pretending it was the funniest thing he'd ever heard, chuckling up a storm. As were the other three men at the table. God help them, Kara thought. Pa was just getting started. "Hey, that's a good one, Des! I'll have to remember it." Pa was happy. Kara exhaled.

While Daniel introduced the other men at the table to Pa, Kara watched from a few feet away, taking in the rest of the room. The tables were filling up. Twin Oaks was disproportionately populated with women, which might have been another reason why the men at Pa's table were more than happy to laugh at anything he said. They were starving, she thought, for "guy" friends.

A kind waitress approached her, offering Kara a seat near Pa's table and a fresh cup of coffee. Kara accepted.

As she sat, half listening to the conversations and half observing the others in the room, she couldn't help admiring how homey Twin Oaks looked. Much care had gone into decorating the main room, a cheerful place with a lot of windows. There were votive candles lining a rough wood mantel that sat above a blazing hearth. Pumpkins, mums and corn stalks filled every corner. And it made her happy to think that, if she couldn't keep Pa at home, at least she could put him in a warm and friendly place. At least she hoped she could. So much was riding on the sale of the house.

After a bit of time, Daniel approached and said in a low voice, "I think he's gonna do just fine, Miss Fitzgerald. You can leave now if you like. I'll keep an eye on him."

"You'll call me if there's a problem?"

Daniel smiled. "Of course. But he seems to be settling in just fine."

Kara liked this man. She took his advice and approached Pa's table, interrupting an animated conversation about the Jets and Giants season prospects.

"Excuse me, gentlemen," then she lowered her voice and turned to Pa. "You okay?" She reminded herself of a nervous mother leaving her child on the first day of school.

"Fine and dandy," he replied with a wink.

"Because I'll be back to see you tomorrow." She watched his face as he processed what she said. "You okay with staying here tonight? With your new friends?"

Daniel broke in. "You'll be just fine, won't you Des?"

Pa smiled and nodded. The waitress began to serve the luncheon entre, shrimp cocktail. Pa's eyes lit up. Kara knew another corny joke was ready to be launched on the unsuspecting victims at the table. "You know, Sports, why I like seafood?" Pa held up one shrimp as if to make his point. Everyone asked "why?" cluelessly ... lambs being led to the slaughter. "Because when I SEE food I EAT it!" That was it. The entire table was yukking it up again. Pa was a hit. Twin Oaks newest class clown.

And on that note, Kara knew it was time to make her exit. She slipped out of the dining room and down the hall to touch base with Mrs. Warren, Twin Oaks' director.

Along the way, passing two laundresses as they pushed carts tidily stacked with fresh sheets and towels, Kara overheard a snipped of their conversation. She pretended to be checking for something in her purse as she listened.

"They won't be comin' out in droves like that when I meet *my* Maker!"

"I hear ya, Sally. And I wouldn't want that kind of fuss anyhow."

Kara smiled. She had learned early in her career how to quickly gain someone's trust, especially when it came to other women.

"I'm sorry I overheard you talking about the reporters. Why were they here?" The women exchanged guarded glances. So much for bonding, though she reasoned that the help was most likely told not to speak about the guests to anyone. Kara took the hint and continued down the hall. She found Mrs. Warren in her office on the phone. There was an air in the room of total chaos ... a far cry from the calm, capable, and confident director of Twin Oaks who Kara met a day earlier.

Catching Kara's eye, she gestured with a long manicured finger that Kara should take a seat while she finished up the call. Kara chose one of the two sumptuous chairs across from the large mahogany desk. A magazine titled "Home Away From Home" was nearby and Kara pretended to be reading it while she listened in to Mrs. Warren's conversation. Clearly not *any* guest, but someone particularly important, had died. But that wasn't what Mrs. Warren was speaking about. Her words were firm to the person on the other end ... something about an unpaid bill and how she'd need to "release" the "guest" from Twin Oaks if it wasn't paid promptly. Kara hoped the same fate would never happen to her. She'd given Twin Oaks a down payment yesterday, every cent in her and Pa's savings account, but she was on the hook for the balance. And that could only be paid once the house was sold.

Mrs. Warren eased off the call. Kara didn't know who she had been talking to, but she felt sorry for them, whoever they were. Money problems. She could identify.

"I'm sorry about that, Miss Fitzgerald." She closed the open folder on her desk. "This is not an ordinary day." She took a sip of tea. "Would you like a cup?" Kara declined. "How is your father adjusting?"

"Well, so far so good. Right now he's enjoying his shrimp cocktail and getting to know some of the men at his table."

"Daniel will make sure he isn't alone, unless he wants to be."

"Daniel's already made my father feel welcome."

Mrs. Warren smiled. "Yes. Daniel has a gift with our guests. He's a gentleman with the women and a man's man with the men."

"Mrs. Warren, about that ruckus outside. Daniel said someone passed?"

Mrs. Warren sighed. "I suppose it will be online in minutes anyway, if it isn't already. Nancy Harding died." She waited for a response from Kara. There was none. "The actress." Then she paused, "before your time." Kara vaguely remembered her parents mentioning the film star from their generation. From what she could recall, only because her mother would watch old movies on the TCM channel, Nancy Harding was a petite blonde with a great figure who was always finding herself in story plots that required her to wear a bikini. "She made a lot of those old beach movies. You might remember. The studio used to pair her up with Biff Daniels. They were quite the couple. On and off the screen."

Kara politely smiled. There was little she could add to the conversation about Nancy Harding other than she didn't seem the type of person to be living at Twin Oaks. Hardly the place for a once glamorous and sexy movie star.

"Why Twin Oaks? What made her decide to live here?" Kara was asking the question that was most likely on everyone's mind.

"When she could have chosen Hollywood or even a posh place in Florida?" Mrs. Warren paused, ready to answer her own question. "I believe she found peace here, away from the glitz and glamour of Hollywood. She was tired of all the pretense. And she was a Jersey girl at heart. Born and raised not far from here."

"Well ... I'm sure she had her reasons," Kara said, but sensed there was more to the story than Mrs. Warren was ready to admit. "Perhaps something kept her here, or someone, who lived nearby."

"Perhaps ..." Mrs. Warren trailed off, then added "Fifty-two. So young to die."

And that was that. Kara wasn't going to get any more information out of Mrs. Warren, if she had any to give. Still, the reporter's wheels were beginning to turn in her head and she wondered if there was a bigger story here. A story she could pitch to her old editor at the *Beacon*.

After leaving Mrs. Warren's office on her way to the car, in a now almost empty parking lot, Kara checked online and saw that, sure enough, there were already several stories about Nancy Harding's death. All read the same, probably taken from her stock biography.

She was a hit in the Eighties, the IT girl of the moment. The darling of the California beach movies and intimate partner to her on screen partner, Biff Daniels. But after Daniels died suddenly in a motorcycle accident, Nancy tried to find happiness with three husbands in short order. None of the marriages turned out well. It was a sad tale of lost love and frustration. Still, there wasn't a hint in any of the articles about why she chose to live out her life, at such a young age, int an assisted living center in New Jersey.

There was a real story here and none of the tabloids were picking up on it. If Nancy Harding wanted to hide from the world, why not hide in Manhattan or Palm Springs or even the Hamptons if she wanted to ditch Hollywood. Why Twin Oaks? THAT was the story. At least, that is what Kara thought.

Chapter Two

"I can't give you your old job back. Heck, I can barely afford to give you an assignment, Kara. My publisher's on my back. Ad revenue's way down." Kara navigated onto the country road leading to the parkway. The moment she left Twin Oaks, she called her former editor, Jack Logan, from the car and asked point blank for a job.

"But it's the kind of story that's perfect for the *Beacon*. Locals would be surprised to learn that they had a famous movie star living all these years nearby and they never knew it. I even have a headline, 'The reluctant star among us.' Now don't tell me *that* won't sell papers … up your circulation numbers. Ad revenue will go through the roof." She exaggerated to make her point. Still, a story about Nancy Harding's reasons for living at Twin Oaks would certainly attract new readers … if only out of curiosity.

"Kara, the cat's already out of the bag. Every online outlet is doing a story on Nancy Harding. Now people know that she was living at Twin Oaks."

"They know THAT she was living there … but they don't know *why*. And I intend to find out."

"You really think they'll plunk down a couple of bucks to read about a secluded movie star?"

"You didn't see all the reporters today at Twin Oaks. But I know the kind of stuff they're going to write. The same old drek taken from her bio. I plan to dig deeper."

"You were at Twin Oaks today?"

"Just came from there. Dropped off my Pa." Then she added, quietly, "His dementia's getting worse."

"Oh …" Jack replied, the extent of his empathy … for anyone.

"Now that the director knows me, I think I can reel her in … I'm sure she'll welcome some positive publicity. Not good for business when a youngish client does on your watch."

"Let me think about it."

"Okay," she smiled, holding back the urge to keep selling the story. But Kara knew from experience that the more she pushed something on Jack Logan, the further he backed away. So she bit her tongue and hoped for the best. That was the way Jack worked. She learned "the Logan Way" back in high school at Nelligan Catholic. Jack was a senior and she was a shy freshman, timidly entering the offices of the school's paper, the *Notch*, one hot September afternoon.

At first he scared her. Jack, being Jack, was far from welcoming, especially of a freshmen … especially of a girl. He kept to himself and was hard on his writers. But Jack's "tough love" eventually transformed Kara into a sharp reporter and a strong writer. She learned to edit her own work and then to re-edit it again before showing it to Jack. Then he'd invariably rip her draft to shreds and she'd 0have to go back and write the story again. But it all paid off. By senior year, Kara was good enough to become editor of the *Notch* herself. Then, after graduation from Montclair State, she applied for a job at the *Beacon*. Jack was its managing editor. And though he admitted in the interview that she was a strong reporter and a solid writer, he almost didn't hire her as he was convinced he could capably edit the struggling daily and cover crime himself. Thankfully, he changed his mind and Kara got the beat, which turned out to be more about petty theft and a few car break-ins than assaults or burglaries. Still, she made that beat her own. And now she wanted it back … or at least the chance to get back on staff. And if that meant starting with an assignment, then so be it. But asking and getting were two vastly different things, especially since she hadn't written a word in the past three years.

"I'll circle back on the Nancy Harding story. It might work," he quipped, surprising Kara. "If the tabloids haven't covered that angle already. But keep in mind, my publisher's put me on a tight budget. Your outline's got to be outstanding."

It was a chance, and Kara jumped at it, especially under the circumstances where things had changed so drastically at local newspapers since she left to care for her parents. People were getting their news, even local news, online. The Covid outbreak made it worse. Locked inside their homes month after month, not able to get out and pick up a coffee and paper at the local newsstand, they got into the habit of getting all their news online. Kara knew that if she was going to get a chance to write for the *Beacon* again, she'd *have* to be outstanding. "Tell you what, Jack. Let me do an outline. On spec. You only have to pay me if you want to go ahead with the story." Then she added, "But I'm confident I can write the kind of piece that will attract new readers."

They finished the call. Kara put her phone down and continued driving while mentally making a list of questions she could ask Mrs. Warren tomorrow when she returned to Twin Oaks. But she no sooner began to make mental notes when the phone buzzed again. It could only be Jack. Kara recalled that this was the way he worked. Talk about something, hang up, then remember another thing he forgot to ask. But she didn't mind. If he was calling with something he forgot to say, that meant he was already thinking of her as part of his team.

"Long time no talk!" she teased.

"Hey ... I just got some news from Cirelli." He was talking about Detective Cirelli, a crusty character and senior detective on the police force. Jack's father and the detective had been cops together, and Jack thought of him as family. When Jack was still a boy, Cirelli took him under his wing after the elder Logan died of a heart attack. If it weren't for the "exclusive" background stories on local crime that the sage detective fed the *Beacon* from time to time, the paper would have folded long ago.

"What's going on?"

"Now keep this under your hat, okay? Cirelli just told me this in the strictest confidence."

"Of course." It was beginning to feel to Kara like old times.

"First of all, the district attorney's office is asking for an autopsy on Nancy Harding."

"That's to be expected, Jack. She was only fifty-two. That's relatively young. And according to Mrs. Warren, that's the director at Twin Oaks, Nancy only got sick in the last week of her life."

"Anyway, the police are looking into foul play."

Kara suddenly felt empty. "Foul play ...?" her voice trailed off. Her first thought was worry. Pa was now at Twin Oaks. Had she done the right thing? Was Pa safe?

"So when you meet with that director, you've gotta get the back story on this. Who came to visit her? What did she have to eat? Was she on drugs and, if so, which ones? Legal or illegal? You know what we're after. And we need it fast ... before the vultures swoop in."

Suddenly her original story, a light and airy piece about the pleasures of a movie star living anonymously in suburban New Jersey was turning into a sleuthing exercise. She was, in a way, back on the crime beat. But was she ready for it?

"Can I still do the outline for my original idea?"

"Yeah ..." she could tell Jack was thinking of something ... then "one might be linked to the other. Maybe Harding was hiding at Twin Oaks ... hiding from someone she feared could do her harm. See what you can get." He hesitated. Kara knew Jack well enough to sense there was something else going on in that mind.

"Jack ... What are you not telling me?"

"Yeah, well ... there *is* something else. But we can't write about it ... not yet."

"I'm listening."

"You remember a guy from Nelligan named Jimmy Mullins? Big basketball star."

Kara gulped. She hadn't heard the name Jimmy Mullins since she left Nelligan nearly fourteen years earlier, but there had been a time when he was the only person she thought about ... day and night. She harbored a huge crush on the handsome, kind, smart and very talented young man. The only thing was that Jimmy Mullins had eyes for another girl ... Cindy Summerfield.

"What about Jimmy?"

"You knew him?"

"Kind of ..." her mind raced back to the first time she fell in love with Jimmy. When he became her hero, though he never knew it. It was February. A brittle cold, grey afternoon. She was a senior. So was he. There was a big basketball game that day. Kara and Katie Hastings had driven to Nelligan for it. When it was over, Kara wanted to hang around the gym in the odd chance she'd "run" into Jimmy. But when she saw Cindy Summerfield, Jimmy's girl, waiting as well, she and Katie decided to leave. Returning to her car in the parking lot, Kara turned the key in the ignition of her old T-bird and suddenly saw what she thought were water vapors oozing up from under the hood. Light, misty steam, or at least it looked that way.

She and Katie ran back to the main building to get water for the radiator. But enroute across the vast parking lot, they suddenly heard a "whoosh!" They spun around to see a fast-growing inferno flashing from the hood. It was Jimmy Mullins and his quick thinking that saved the day. The basketball star, fresh from the locker room, kicked in the glass over the fire extinguisher and ran out to the burning car to get the blaze under control. When the fire trucks finally arrived, the chief told Jimmy that, had he not been so quick to take charge of the situation, the fire would have spread to other cars with disastrous and possibly fatal results.

After that day, Kara was more in love with Jimmy Mullins then ever. Though he would never know it.

"What about Jimmy?" she heard her voice quiver. Something told her it wasn't going to be good news.

"Cirelli called to say that some corporate execs on a hike up at the Hague mansion found Jimmy's body on a trail. Early this morning." He allowed a moment for it to sink in.

"Jimmy's dead? Was it a heart attack?"

"No. Murdered." Kara couldn't move her lips to respond. "Kara? You there?"

"What happened?"

"Stabbed. Eight times. No leads. Other than the people who were with him on the retreat."

"Retreat?"

"Yeah. Three married couples. Some knew Jimmy from Nelligan." He paused. "Listen, Kara, I'm only telling you this in case you hear anything through the grapevine. But Cirelli asked that we not print a word until he gives us the okay."

"Is anyone in custody?"

"No. But he's talking with the couples from the retreat. Between you and me, the police consider them persons of interest. Other than them, the place was empty. Only a caretaker and a maid. So it had to be one of them with an axe to grind."

"But maybe it wasn't one of them. Maybe someone else had it in for Jimmy … though I don't know why."

"The place had no other guests that weekend."

"Okay … I don't stay in touch with anyone from Nelligan, but if I hear anything through the grapevine …"

"Yeah. That would be great."

"But don't the police want our help? I mean, we could break the story and maybe someone saw something." She realized she was suddenly talking about an old friend as if he were a stranger. It hadn't sunk in yet that this was her hero, Jimmy Mullins, the kindest person, other than her parents, she'd ever known.

"No. Cirelli was adamant. We can't go to print on this … not yet." For Jack to hold back on a potentially huge story was out of character. There had to be more to it. "I just thought you should know … he was in your class and all." Jack paused.

"But maybe the public can help."

"No … no stories … yet. Cirelli said the Archdiocese is worried about copycats …nutjobs comin' out of the woodwork to kill priests."

Kara did a mental doubletake. "Jimmy was a priest?" In her mind, she had always seen Jimmy and Cindy Summerfield as married, living happily ever after with their family of good-looking, athletic, kind-hearted kids. It was the path that the popular people at Nelligan were supposed to take. Date. Marry. Kids. Wonderful life.

"Yeah. He was a priest at some parish in the hood. Tryin' to bring gang members to Jesus. That's what you get for bein' a do-gooder."

"But you said he was on a marriage retreat?"

"Yeah. Cirelli said he was doin' a favor for some Nelligan grads. Couples in trouble, I guess. Makes you glad you never married, ey? They were the only ones with him that weekend.

"Maybe one of the gang members did it. Those guys can be ruthless."

"Yeah … but at a place like the Hague mansion, I mean, it's pretty upscale … anyone with even a tattoo would stand out like Zorro at a First Communion. If you get my drift."

"How … when did it happen?"

"Early. Around six-thirty. Mullins was in jogging clothes but under his shirt he was wearin' his Roman collar."

"That means he might have been expecting to pray with someone … or hear their confession … or advise them." Kara thought aloud.

"You're sayin' he was on the job, even when out jogging."

"He might have been. But what could possibly be the motive? Money? Priests have no money."

Kara was still trying to wrap her head around Jimmy Mullins becoming a priest, much less that he was dead. She tried to visualize where it took place. Her mind raced back to her one and only time visiting the Hague mansion. It was before it became a fancy hotel and conference center. Back when the wealthy Hague family loaned it out to civic groups. She was on a camping trip with the Girl Scouts. During the day, the trails and scenery were gorgeous, wrapped in nature and endless meanderings through brush and bramble and jagged cliffs. But at night, as she and her friends huddled together in their camping tent, it was frightening. The sounds of nature took over and terrified the patch of suburban girls who weren't used to growls and owls sounding off in the black night.

"Who knows the motive. I'm only tellin' you this because you might hear somethin' … being that you were in Mullins' class. If we can pick up some info to feed Cirelli … hey, always good to trade favors with the police, right?"

"Got it." Kara remembered how the game was played. Tit for tat. An exchange of information and access between cops and reporters. But no sooner did they end the phone call when the reality of what Jack just told her sunk in. This wasn't some random act of violence against a stranger. This was murder … against the boy she adored and kept alive in her mind all these years since high school ended. Her hero … who always seemed to be at the right place at the right time to keep her safe. If only she had been around to repay the favor. But now it was over. Jimmy was gone. To heaven. Never to return to earth. Never to save the day for her again. . And though she hadn't seen him in fourteen years, she could no longer hold out hope that, out of the blue, he'd possibly, one day, suddenly appear.

With this new reality settling over her, Kara began to shake. She shook so violently and relentlessly that she needed to get off the call and pull the Civic to the side of the road. There, after many deep breaths, she was able to settle her nerves … just. Enough to move from shock to grief with no other emotion in between. And in that moment, Kara broke down. She allowed the tears to flow as she covered her face in her hands, sobbing uncontrollably.

Chapter Three

Nothing could feel worse than how Kara felt at this moment. All the energy in her limbs left her. But, as the whizz of cars sped by, she knew she couldn't just sit there on the side of the road and wallow in grief. Slowly, she pulled the Civic back onto the highway. She drove, but her mind was on autopilot as she navigated her way back home, having that jolt of amazement, and fear, when she realized she was suddenly pulling into her driveway and hadn't remembered a thing about the ride home.

Home. It was not going to be home for long. But for now, the tiny Cape Cod with the patch of green and the dusty rose hydrangeas guarding the front stoop was all hers. As she headed up the steps, Kara suddenly realized that the "For Sale" sign Connie Belford replaced in front now had a sticker diagonally across it saying "Under Contract." The feeling was bittersweet. Sweet in that it meant the Asian couple made an offer and she'd have the money in time to pay the rest of Pa's bill at Twin Oaks. And bitter in that she'd have to leave the only home she'd ever known. Soon it would be time to pack up and go … but *where* she would go, she had no idea.

Inside, Kara locked the front door behind her and went straight to the kitchen to make herself a strong cup of tea. As she waited for the kettle to boil, she jumped into the shower to wash away the day. The steamy cocoon engulfed her like a comforting blanket. She could have stayed there for hours if she didn't hear the shrill sound to remind her that her tea water was ready. Quickly, she stepped out, toweled off, put on her most comfy sweats and headed down to the kitchen.

But no amount of tea could take away the pain that lingered in her heart. Jimmy Mullins was gone. And whoever had the audacity to take his life robbed both her and the rest of the human race from one of the truly good ones.

As she sipped the tea, Kara recalled another memory when Jimmy came to her rescue. It was a night shortly after graduation from Nelligan. She and Katie Hastings decided to celebrate with a burger at Moran's, a local pub. As neither had cars, they walked the half mile to Moran's in daylight, but by the time they were leaving, it was half past ten and suddenly the once friendly side roads cast an ominous spell in the darkness. So they called for an Uber lift and waited out front.

The scene was like most local pubs after the patrons have had a few too many. While Kara and Katie weren't drinkers, everyone else was. One guy in particular, a burly fellow, burst out of the place and slobbered over to her and Katie. At first. nobody paid him any mind, even when the drunk began to harass the young women. Earlier, he had approached them, coming on to Kara in particular. Now, as he closed in, his hot breath reeked of alcohol, his eyes blurred. Kara tried to be polite but made it clear that she wasn't interested. The drunk didn't care. Offended that his attentions were being rebuked, he stepped up his campaign of obnoxious behavior, pressing closer to Kara. Suddenly his thick body had her pinned against a parked car.

"I have a boyfriend," she lied, trying to exert as much control as she could into the situation … without effect. And, with several other young men in the vicinity, it appeared immediately that none of them wanted to tussle with the burly, surly drunk. Chivalry was on life support. She and Katie knew they were on their own. Kara wished she knew a few choice martial arts moves or had a can of mace in her possession as the drunk pressed tighter, nearly suffocating her. His hands took over, sliding down her waist, coming perilously close to the bottom of her skirt. Kara was walking a tightrope. If she was too quiet he'd take her timidity as a "yes" and if she was too harsh he'd step up his aggression.

"I said leave me alone," she inserted in a strong voice. He wasn't listening.

Stay calm, she told herself. And she prayed. "Holy Mother Mary, help me. Help me, please."

"I said stop!" she heard her voice, firm but still modulated with fear. Then Katie inched her way close enough to take her stiletto, squeeze her leg between his and Kara's and press the spikey heel firmly into the top of his shoe, which luckily was a canvas sneaker, cutting into his instep and causing him to wince with pain. In a second, he released his grip, allowing a sliver of space for Kara to slip away.

At that moment, as if heaven sent, she heard "Kara …Get in!" It was Jimmy. He had been out on a date with Cindy. They nearly drove past the pub when he spotted his friend in trouble. Now he was standing next to the back seat of his old Mustang, steering the girls to safety.

Before the drunk could figure out what was going on, Jimmy was behind the wheel again and the Mustang sped away.

"You girls okay?" Jimmy asked as they fled the scene.

"Yes," Kara caught her breath. "Now we are. That guy was terrifying."

They drove the rest of the way in silence. The girls were still shell-shocked. Jimmy dropped Katie off first, then dropped Kara at her house. Nothing more was said. Nothing needed to be said, except Kara's profound "thank you" and then he drove off. He and Cindy. Having saved her ... again. To Kara Fitzgerald, Jimmy Mullins was now her *Super*hero and Guardian Angel in one.

Lost in thought, Kara realized she was dunking the tea bag in and out of the water. She went to the fridge to get the milk. Then she took her teacup out to the back patio. The weather was comfortable, one of the last lovely days of October before a full autumn blast blew in. She hoped the fresh air and the tea would bring comfort. Little did she realize that comfort, or a bit of it, was about to take another form.

It was dusk. The time of day that plays tricks on the eyes. Kara sat on one of the wrought iron chairs at the round glass table and listened to the sounds of nature. A bird chirp. A cricket. Where had the day gone, she wondered. And then she answered her own question. The day slipped away as quickly as her heart lost bits of itself. First separating from her beloved Pa; worrying for him. And then the horrific news about Jimmy. That's where it had gone. Swallowed up by worry and grief.

Deep in her thoughts, Kara nearly jumped out of the chair when she suddenly felt a gentle "something" rubbing up against her ankle. She looked down and saw her ... the tiny grey intruder who decided Kara was her new best friend. Scruffy. Bone thin. But chock full of charm.

"Where did *you* come from?" The little cat kept rubbing against her leg. She leaned down and caressed its tufted fur. It instantly turned onto its back, as if expecting a belly rub. For the moment, all worries about Pa and sadness about Jimmy left her spirit. "You're little and you're grey. Can I call you Little Grey?"

"I'd prefer you call me Joe." Startled, Kara looked up to see a smiling, handsome man. He seemed to appear out of nowhere. Cloaked in the backdrop of a setting sun, Kara could still make out his pearly white teeth and the glisten in his brown eyes. "I'm putting out food for them. Over in our yard," he nodded to the house behind Kara's. "Took a headcount and figured she wondered off."

"Is she yours?"

"No. I'm only feeding her, and a few others. Feral cats. My mother is actually their benefactor but as I'm housesitting while my folks are in Florida …."

"*You're* temporarily their caretaker," Kara smiled, the first time she smiled all day.

"That's it." He had a kind face.

"You're new to the neighborhood?"

"No. Actually, I've lived here my whole life."

Kara was taken aback. Why hadn't she ever met this handsome guy before? She certainly would have noticed. "I'm Joe. Joe Collins." He extended his hand. It was calloused. The way Pa's used to feel when he worked in construction.

"I can't believe we were neighbors all this time and never met," Kara said as she looked into his eyes framed by thick brown brows. Then she looked quickly away, not wanting to stare. But it was hard not to … stare, that is. .

"Well I remember *you*." he smiled. "I used to see you waiting for the bus in your Nelligan uniform."

"You …" Kara was taken off guard.

"I went to Richmond. My grades weren't good enough for Nelligan."

"And you've lived here all this time?"

"No. Spent twelve years in the Navy after high school then the last two in construction. My company just finished renovating the office building over on Fifth Street."

"I know that building. You did that?"

He smiled. "Me and my guys." It was a complete restoration. Kara had driven past the location and admired how the workers were staying true to the original design. With Pa in construction, she appreciated fine workmanship.

"You know my Pa used to work in construction. He did a lot of restoration work," she said proudly.

"Really? I'd like to talk with him about it … if he has the time."

"Oh, he's got nothing but time," she joked to herself, knowing Joe had no idea what she meant.

"He's retired?"

"You could say that. Today I had to admit him to Twin Oaks. The assisted living center."

"Oh … I just saw on the news that someone from there died … somebody famous … uh …"

"Nancy Harding."

"Yeah. That's it. Never heard of her." He paused to pick up the kitten. "Anyway, I hope I can meet your Pa sometime. Talk shop, you know?"

"He'd like that."

"Well, we'll be going," he gestured to the tiny furry ball in his large hands.

"Uh … do you think I can have her?" Kara heard herself say, not thinking for a moment about whether she'd be able to take a kitten to her new home … wherever that would be.

"Sure. Of course." He smiled, then added, "I can fix you up with a few cans of cat food and a bag of litter." Then he looked down at the little cat resting in the crook of Kara's arm. "I think *she* actually chose *you*!"

"I think you're right," Kara smiled. "And thank you for the food and litter. Let me know what it costs."

"Oh, no charge. My mother wouldn't hear of it. She'll be glad to know this little lady is going to a good home." Then he added, "I'll drop the stuff off at your patio door in a little while. After I feed the others. If I wait too much longer, they may start picketing."

"Well just tell them that beggars can't be choosers."

"I tried that. It didn't work." He smiled and extended his hand. "Nice to meet you, Kara"

"Nice to meet you, Joe." She paused. "You already know my name?"

"My bus would pass your bus stop every morning. I used to see you out there waiting in your navy and tan plaid skirt, that tan blazer and those saddle shoes."

She blushed and rolled her eyes. "Let's just say the nun who designed that ensemble wasn't named Stella McCartney!"

He chuckled. "I liked how you looked." His eyes met hers. They were smiling. "Hope I see you again … soon." Then he walked off. Kara watched him head back toward his house, swallowed up in the grey of dusk and she wondered to herself, "Where has this Joe Collins been

all my life?"

Chapter Four

October sunrises are almost as beautiful as they are in May. Brilliant strands of soft gold pierced through a crack in the draperies that covered the patio door casting a gentle, dusty beam across the living room. Kara woke up on the couch, slowly. It had been her first night, ever, alone in the house and she spent it sleeping in the living room near the lingering aroma of Pa's aftershave that wafted from his favorite wing chair. Though she had no reason to expect an intruder, Kara kept an old baseball bat nearby, just "in case." Little Grey curled up in the crook of her knees.

As she lay on the couch, collecting her thoughts, she played back yesterday … checking Pa into Twin Oaks; getting an assignment, or *almost* an assignment, from Jack' finding out about Jimmy's murder' receiving an offer on the house' adopting a cat and meeting Joe. A rollercoaster of emotional ups and downs. Thankfully, Little Grey was a distraction. The kitten was pawing Kara's favorite pair of sweats, leaving pulls and tiny dents in the soft cotton.

"I own a cat!" the absurdity of taking on responsibility for a tiny living being at such an unsteady chapter in her life suddenly hit her. But she had no time to contemplate the commitment. It was time to get off the couch and go to the patio door. Opening the draperies to let in the morning light, Kara saw several cans of cat food and a large bag of kitty litter waiting. Joe had come through.

Not only had he come through with provisions, but Kara spotted in his yard something she never noticed before. Joe was building a shed. Not any shed, but from what she could see, it was equipped with cubbyholes and ramps that led to windowless windows. Already, some of the strays he was feeding had moved in. *He's making a shelter for them*, she thought … and the idea of it made her smile.

Back in the kitchen, Kara filled the kettle and put it on the stove to make her first cup of what would likely be a three-cup morning of tea. Then she popped open a can of cat food and placed it on an old kitchen plate, one with trio of fairy princesses on it, a souvenir from a trip to Disneyworld, long, long ago.

As she watched Little Grey lick away at her breakfast, Kara got a teacup out of the cupboard and a bag of Lipton's. Then her phone buzzed. The caller I.D. read *Connie Belford.* Kara let the call go to message. Connie was not the kind of person you wanted to start your day with … she was an "after eleven," meaning that she was one of those people whose voice and manner were better left to later on in the day when one's psyche was more amenable to harsh sounds.

"Kaaa-rahh ... I have great news!" The message began. Kara poured boiling water over the teabag and braced herself as she took in Connie's less-than-dulcet tones. " Are you awake, Doll? Because it's a win-win!." A *"win-win?"* Connie had a way of pulling you into her drama. Kara gave in and picked up.

"Hi Connie," She tried to sound friendly, but in truth, her voice gave away her dislike for the pushy realtor. Still, it was Connie's aggressive tactics that made her one of the best realtors in town. And she needed Connie's force to sell an old, outdated house for top dollar. "I saw the Under Contract sticker. Did their offer meet my asking price?" It was the million dollar question. If Kara didn't get her price for the house, she wouldn't be able to keep Pa at Twin Oaks.

"Yes, Doll. We have a healthy off-a." Connie was setting her up and Kara knew it. "The Orientals offered a fair price … below but still presentable."

"How presentable?"

"Only ten thousand *below* …" Connie said matter-of-factly with the inference that Kara would be a fool not to accept the low-ball figure. "A bird in the hand, Ka-ra …"

"Can't you get them to meet my asking price? Ten thousand might not seem like much to you but it's a great deal to me. Without it I won't have enough to find myself a new place."

Connie sighed. "It's a fair off-a, Ka-ra. You really want me to go back to them and say no?"

"I'd like you to ask them to meet my price."

"They won't. They said that's their final off-a." She feigned impatience, "If you must know, they asked if I can find them other houses to look at just in case you turned them down."

Kara knew the wily realtor had her over a barrel. Plus, it was a buyers' market. And the house needed some work to bring it into the Twenty-first century. If she turned down the Asian couple's offer, she could be waiting a year to sell the house at her asking price. She heard about that happening to other people. Unfortunately, time was not on her side and that was not an option.

Connie continued, "No offense, Doll, but your house is a fixer-upp-a. And young couples today insist on move-in ready. These people are willing to pay under value so they can do the upgrades themselves."

Connie's words, that the potential buyers were "willing" hit Kara hard. She had always loved this house, even with its quirky kitchen cabinets and the creaks that told you someone was in the upstairs hallway. It was old but lovable and warm and cozy, especially at Christmastime. To think of strangers coming in and making so-called "upgrades" was a bitter pill to swallow.

"Let me think about it."

"Ka-ra, you know me, I'm on your side. But you need a sale ..."

Kara knew she was between a rock and a hard place. "Tell them I'll accept their offer."

She hung up the phone and knew that it was now down to the wire. The good news was that she'd be able to pay Twin Oaks for Pa's care. The bad news was that she had to find a decent paying job and a new place to live. Pronto.

Chapter Five

The rooster clock above the kitchen sink read seven thirty, still too early to visit Pa. But not too early to make a "to do" list. Kara knew she'd have to use all her will power to get it in gear, to move on. So she did what she always did when she needed self motivation. She made a "to do" list. It was a mental map of her day, to get her started on her Nancy Harding story … and to also get her moving toward "the big move."

Since visiting hours at Twin Oaks didn't start for another hour and a half, Kara thought she might still go there early on the off chance Mrs. Warren was available. She wanted to get some insights about Nancy Harding. Things about her habits, any friends she made at Twin Oaks, basically anything that would give the Beacon's readers more insight into why Nancy chose to live in such a place.

And as Mrs. Warren was most likely guarded about all of her "guests," Kara knew she'd need to pour on the charm if she was going to convince her that such a story would be good publicity. Kara planned to start with flattery. It always worked. She'd pitch the story as one that would highlight all the positive reasons why someone like Nancy Harding, a once glittering Hollywood star, would choose seclusion and serenity. Naturally, the piece would also touch on Nancy's past, her ex-husbands and lovers, her faded beauty … but those things were all the more reason why she would search for peace and comfort far away from Hollywood.

Of course, Kara knew Mrs. Warren would be protective of her staff. She wouldn't be a good director if she weren't. But Kara knew she could persuade her that the article would focus more on the superior care all of the guests at Twin Oaks receive, and less on the why … why

someone of only fifty-two would suddenly die in their care.

She checked the time. Still too early to leave for Twin Oaks. So she did a cursory search

online for the obituaries and articles that came out yesterday. Every story read the same. Hers

would be different. It had to be different so it would sell papers, boost Jack's circulation numbers

and justify him putting her back on staff. .

Kara came upon an old interview with Nancy that appeared in the magazine *Good

Housekeeping.* It ran ten years ago. In it, Nancy was surprisingly candid, talking about her early

life growing up poor in Jersey City. The story was all rah-rah about how the penniless young

actress pulled herself up by her bootstraps and took modelling jobs in Manhattan which quickly

led to Hollywood movie roles. Strangely, while she made her fortune wearing very few items of

clothing, Nancy was quoted as saying that she resented being cast as a "sex symbol."

Another interview, done when Nancy was at the height of her fame and on her third

husband, discussed her "one true love," which was Biff Daniels, her frequent co-star who died

tragically in a motorcycle accident nineteen years ago, the same year Nancy entered Twin Oaks.

Kara guessed it was more than a coincidence. Perhaps, Kara wondered, losing Biff was what sent

Nancy into seclusion.

Then there was the story in the *New York Post* from two years ago that was captioned

"Guess who?" and showed a recent photo of Nancy, snapped outside what appeared to be a

bakery, shoving a cupcake into her mouth. She was wearing oversized grey sweats, her hair

frazzled and frizzy, her face paunchy and lined and her shape disproportionately far from her

once perfect size two.

Kara suddenly felt a pang of compassion for the lost and lonely star. Nancy Harding had clearly given up on life when there was so much life left to live.

She returned her attention to the *Good Housekeeping* interview. There was something in it that had caught her eye. A question to Nancy by the interviewer. It was in bold italic font and set apart from the copy. ***"Any regrets?"*** To which Nancy answered that she regretted not being closer to her "loved ones." What loved ones? Kara wondered. When she reread the piece, Kara realized that Nancy had no siblings, three ex-husbands who were all, in her own words, "bastards," and her parents were long dead. The only mention of a family member was her nephew, the former child actor, Ricky Wexner. He was living in Florida at the time. Kara did a quick Google search and found an address for an R. Wexner in the Boca Raton area.

She closed up her laptop and downed the last of her third cup of tea. Time to see Mrs. Warren then look in on Pa. She dressed quickly in jeans, then grabbed her notebook and left.

The drive to Twin Oaks on a sunny fall morning was lovely. Once the Civic turned onto the long, oak-lined road leading to the main gate, Kara felt instantly at peace. There *was* something special about this place, she thought, and she kind of understood why Nancy would choose to live here.

Arriving to the aroma of bacon frying, Kara detoured to take a quick look into the dining room. Sure enough, she found Pa, all clean shaven and dressed for the day, happily sipping tea, and sitting at the same table as yesterday with his new friends.

He was clearly in his element. After giving him a quick kiss on the cheek and getting assurance from Daniel that all went well last night and he "slept like a baby," Kara headed down the hall to see Mrs. Warren, passing orderlies, maids and bed-ridden guests along the way.

"Has all the hoopla from yesterday died down?" Kara smiled as she stood in the doorframe of the posh mahogany office. Mrs. Warren looked up from her desk and returned a smile, a good sign.

"Please come in, Miss Fitzgerald. Help yourself to some coffee," she gestured to the silver urn and white cups on a sideboard. "And yes, things are slowly getting back to normal."

They broke the ice, talking about Pa and his adjustment, which Mrs. Warren agreed was going well. Then Kara segued into her story pitch.

"I read this morning in an old article that Nancy Harding regretted not being closer to her loved ones. But the stories I read only mentioned a nephew. Some child actor."

"Yes. Ricky Wexner. But he's an adult now." Mrs. Warren glanced down at her cell phone. "He never came to visit his aunt. Until recently ..."

"Oh?"

"Yes. Out of the blue he suddenly began to show up during the final weeks of her life."

"That must have made her happy."

"To the contrary. Oh, I think she liked having a visitor, but he was clearly under the influence of something. After a few visits, and I'm sure a few checks passed from her to him, she insisted he check into a rehabilitation facility in Florida."

"And ... did he go .... to rehab?"

"Eventually. But not right away. Nancy made it non-negotiable or she threatened to cut him out of her will."

"He must have had a severe addiction for Miss Harding to make that kind of threat."

"Yes, he did. You could tell just by looking at the man. Sunken eyes. Dry, pale complexion. Skinny as a rail. But like all addicts, he knew the art of manipulation … especially of his aunt. Poured on the charm." She paused to take a sip of coffee. "I know she sent him money every month. I know because I mailed the checks. But I guess it wasn't good enough. He came in person to collect more." Mrs. Warren clearly didn't like Ricky Warren.

"And she gave it to him?"

"Like I said … he could manipulate her." Another pause. Another sip. "Seems like they had arguments every time he visited."

"But you said he rarely visited."

"Yes. He stayed away for the nineteen years she lived here. No phone calls. No birthday or Christmas cards. No nothing. Then he suddenly shows up looking for cash."

"And when she threatened to take him out of her will, did she?"

"I don't know." Mrs. Warren looked off.

"Do you know if Ricky Wexner ever went to rehab?'

"Well, I assume he agreed to it. For a few days, they seemed to have made a truce of sorts. There was no more arguing, at least from what we could hear. And he kept bringing her cupcakes every day." She paused and smiled wistfully, "Nancy had a preference for the carrot cake cupcakes they sell at Vitale's."

"I know Vitale's. Delicious cakes ... and very expensive."

Mrs. Warren smiled. "Yes, I got my daughter's birthday cake there. Anyway, he brought at least half a dozen Vitale's cupcakes every day, even though he knew she was a diabetic and on insulin. I mean, bringing one cupcake would have been fine, I suppose, but six! And she devoured them." She added. "I disliked him for tempting her like that."

"And you're sure he knew she was a diabetic?"

"Yes. Absolutely. I told him. So did Daniel. He just smiled, like he was laughing at us."

"You believe he was trying to harm his aunt?"

Mrs. Warren suddenly flushed with anger. "You mean do I think he was trying to send his aunt to an early grave so he could get his hands on her money?"

"I was simply thinking …"

"I don't know, Miss Fitzgerald." Then she stopped, the way people do when they realize they said too much. "Please don't repeat what I just said. I have no proof there was any ill will. I'm just saying …"

"No, no, I understand," Kara knew she touched a nerve. "But you felt he didn't treat his aunt the way she deserved to be treated."

"I don't think he really loved her. But I have no proof that he intentionally tried to harm her. He was, is an addict. Addicts do not think straight. They only think of their next fix. The cupcakes were his way of buttering her up so he could get the cash he came for."

"If I were you I'd be thinking the same thing, Mrs. Warren. "But Nancy clearly found something here at Twin Oaks that made her felt comfortable and secure for nineteen years, and I'd like to write a story for the *Beacon* about it. I occasionally write feature stories for them."

Kara paused to allow Mrs. Warren to digest her proposal. "Would you mind if I had some of that coffee?" Kara gestured to the silver urn and cups on the side bar.

"Of course." Mrs. Warren began to sift through some files on her desk. "We could certainly use a positive piece. We were bombarded yesterday with calls from relatives of our guests. They all jumped to the conclusion that Nancy died of suspicious causes."

"Because she was only fifty-two."

"Yes." Mrs. Warren opened one of the folders and pulled out a photo of Nancy then slid it across the desk. It was the same photo Kara had seen in the *NY Post*, of a very overweight Nancy shoving a cupcake in her mouth. Only this was a full body shot showing Nancy needing a cane.

"How did she get this way? I mean, she once had everything."

"Everything except someone to love her. And we tried here to make her feel like family. All of the staff. As we do for all our guests." Then she said quietly, "But I don't think she ever completely trusted anyone."

"Even Biff Daniels?"

"You're referring to the boyfriend? Well, she did tell me once that he was the love of her life. And I do think that his tragic death started her decline."

"He died in a motorcycle crash?"

"Yes. But at the time they were no longer a couple. I believe he cheated on her, just like the others. But she always held a torch for that guy, even after she married three other men."

Kara found her moment. "Mrs. Warren, my story would focus on the care Nancy received here at Twin Oaks and the family that your staff provided her." She paused. "But I'd also have to include the part about Nancy's nephew and how he only started visiting her during her final days." She paused. "That Nancy wanted him to go into rehab."

"But why would you need to include such a thing?"

"Firstly, because it's a fact. And second, because it will likely come out in one of the online tabloids only they will infer all sorts of things … mostly lies."

"Things like what?"

"Oh, you know how they take something and blow it out of proportion. They could suggest that Nancy took her own life."

"But she didn't."

"Or that the nephew intentionally brought cupcakes knowing his aunt was trying to watch what she ate."

"She was a diabetic."

"And her nephew knew it?"

"I told him so. As did Daniel. But it didn't seem to matter to him. His goal was to sweeten the pot, as they say. To get money out of his aunt at any cost."

Kara took a sip of coffee. "So … would you allow me to write the story? I'll send you my first draft for your review. None of the online pubs will do that. They'll print whatever they want without backing up the facts."

Mrs. Warren drew in a breath. "I understand your point, Miss Fitzgerald. And we could certainly use a positive story about all the fine things we provide for our guests … but I'm still uncertain about bringing in the part about Nancy's nephew."

"But he's part of the story … and this is the crime reporter in me, but if he did intentionally bring those cupcakes knowing that his aunt was diabetic and could go into shock from the sugar overload, then won't it be better if my story addresses the fine care Nancy received here for nineteen years, nineteen years without a single incident, before Ricky Wexner arrived on the scene. Whether his arrival was a coincidence with Nancy's sudden demise or not, we don't want the public to put the onus on your staff."

Kara knew her argument was sound. She rested her case. And before she finished her cup of coffee, Mrs. Warren was on board with the story.

Kara left Mrs. Warren's office with a head full of notes, ready to start writing. But before she went home to her laptop, she headed back to the dining room to say goodbye to Pa. Nearly there, she almost collided with a familiar face.

"Detective?" Detective Corelli's resting face looked perennially tired. "It's Kara. Kara Fitzgerald." His pale eyes lit up and he offered a weak smile.

"Kara! Of course! It's been ages. How are you?"

"I'm fine, thank you. I was just speaking with Mrs. Warren." He looked at her suspiciously. "I checked my father in here yesterday."

"Your father? Is he not well?"

"Dementia."

"Oh, I'm sorry to hear that. But they have a good reputation for that kind of thing."

"Yes. He arrived in the middle of all the Nancy Harding hoopla." Then: "Is there any follow-up, Detective? Anything we can print in the *Beacon*?"

"No," he was terse. It was not his style and that told Kara that something was amiss.

"I heard about Father Mullins."

"Kara, I told Jack Logan that we cannot put anything in the press. I only gave him a heads up because he was likely to get wind of it through his sources and …"

"No. I understand." Kara was about to use an old reporting trick … leveraging her knowledge of Jimmy for information about Nancy Harding … if there was any. "It's just that I went to Nelligan with Jimmy and, well, he was a dear friend."

"I'm so sorry for his folks. Good people."

"But getting back to Nancy. Did you get the autopsy report back? I understand she was a diabetic."

"You're writing about this now?"

"I'm doing a piece. Yes." She paused. "I'm sure you're doing an autopsy."

"We are."

"And?"

The detective had been in the game long enough to know that he could enlist the public's help through the press. It was a mutually beneficial relationship. The *Beacon* got an exclusive, a scoop from the police and the police got a story that might lead to more leads in a case.

"And we found arsenic in her system."

"Arsenic!"

"That's what I've come to talk about with Mrs. Warren."

"From something she ate …"

"We're investigating what she ate."

"And the cupcakes that her nephew brought her."

"I have two officers on their way down to Boca right now to question Wexner."

"May I print this?" Kara found that asking permission to print something was just a polite way of confirming what she already intended to print.

"Yes. We're gonna need the public's help on this one. Somebody, maybe the nephew and maybe not, with access to Nancy Harding wanted to see her dead." The detective suddenly clammed up. "Hey, good seeing you, Kara." He grazed her upper arm in a fatherly way. "Hope it all goes well with your Dad."

Kara high tailed it back to her car. She couldn't wait to get on her cell to tell Jack. This was turning into his kind of story.

Chapter Six

Kara called Jack's line the moment she got into her car but it was busy, per usual. As she started the car, she allowed what she just learned about Nancy to sink in.

In the past, when she covered crime for the Beacon, she was usually assigned to stories about car break-ins or home burglaries. There were no murders on her beat. Now she was looking at two. And she wasn't sure if it all sank in yet.

What ever could possess anyone to snuff out the precious life of anyone else? It just wasn't the kind of thing that Kara allowed herself to contemplate. Her own life was full of love. Love for her mother as she cared for her in those final days. Love for her Pa as she tried to make him safe and comfortable at Twin Oaks. Love was what guided her every action. And murder was just something that was the farthest thing from love.

She remembered reading a holy card that came from a relative after her mother died. The card said, "our loved ones are only on loan to us." How true, she thought. Nobody in our lives is a guarantee. And, like Detective Cirelli, she felt for Jimmy's parents who were paying back their loan from God, paid in full after only thirty-two years with their precious son.

Her heart now heavy, Kara turned off the car and went back into Twin Oaks. She found Pa, still in the dining room, now enjoying a hearty breakfast of oatmeal and a fried egg, holding court with his new buddies. And it made her smile. She had done the right thing, whatever the cost in money and emotion to her.

After giving him a kiss on the cheek, a kiss that didn't interrupt Pa's bad joke telling, Kara spotted Daniel seated in the far corner, keeping watch on everything. He waved her over.

"Good morning, Miss Fitzgerald!" Daniel stood. "May we offer you breakfast?"

"No, but thank you." She looked over at Pa. "I thought I was coming here to comfort him but from what I can see he needs no comforting. I haven't seen him this happy since before my mother got ill … and that was three years ago. He's already acting like his old self."

"I'm mighty glad to hear that."

"And no wandering last night?"

"Not once," then Daniel added, "and don't you worry about that. If he does decide to take a stroll, our night staff will guide him right back to his bed."

"I'm glad to hear that. But I do have one concern. I noticed there isn't a security guard posted at any of the doors."

"Now don't you worry, Miss Fitzgerald. All the doors are locked and bolted at night. Nobody gets in or out. And during the day, well, there are so many staffers on duty that we know everything that's going on."

"Yes, but in the daytime anyone could simply come in … *anyone* …"

Daniel's perennial smile suddenly disappeared. "Ricky Warren was a relative of a guest here." He said firmly. "We cannot prevent visitors if they have a guest's approval." Then he changed back to his usual friendly demeanor. "Miss Fitzgerald, our founder didn't want this place to be like a nursing home. You know, all stink and indifference. She wanted it to feel like a real home. And people don't have security guards in their real homes.

"And this policy works?"

"We've never had a problem." His tone was abrupt. End of discussion. Kara had clearly pinched a nerve.

Chapter Seven

"Good work, Fitz!" Jack was in a rare mood. He actually sounded happy. Kara knew it wouldn't last. "Now go write the story and be sure to point the finger at Wexner."

"Jack, I can write about the results of the autopsy, but I can't point the finger at Wexner or anyone else for that matter. The *Beacon* could be sued for defamation. And Detective Cirelli would never trust me with another scoop."

"So what are you gonna write?" He was back to his "normal" agitated self.

"I'm going to write the facts. That Nancy moved into Twin Oaks for the peace and security it provided. That she thought of the staff as her family. And that, unfortunately, it appears that her death was due to foul play, traceable to some poisoned cupcakes that arrived on the front stoop with her name on the bakery box."

"That's not gonna cut it."

Kara held her ground. "It's the truth. And we won't get sued … unless you think your publisher would like to be sued by Ricky Wexner for defamation?" He ignored her.

"What about the bakery?"

"Vitale's? I'll give them a call but I'm sure the police have already interrogated them. Detective Cirelli is also sending some officers down to the rehab facility in Boca where Wexner is currently living."

"So Wexner IS the guy."

"He's a person of interest. That doesn't mean he's a killer."

"Sounds like he is."

"No … none of the cupcakes that Wexner brought on his visits to his aunt were poisoned. It's the ones that arrived on the front stoop, some time during the night, AFTER he returned to Boca. Someone who knew his pattern could be trying to frame him."

"What's this about cupcakes on a stoop?"

"Never mind. I'll put it all in my first draft." She left out the part about sending the draft to him AFTER Mrs. Warren saw it first. It was the right thing to do. And a promise she intended to keep … and not tell Jack about.

She hung up and turned the Civic onto the long drive that led through the tall pines, the majestic oaks and the brilliant sugar maples that peopled Twin Oaks' grounds. It was truly a gorgeous place, but Kara wondered if any of the guests ever enjoyed the beautiful environs. She tended to think not. Most were bed ridden or too frail to get around without the aid of a wheelchair, making it unlikely that any of them was involved in Nancy's murder. But the staff? She wondered.

As Kara eased the Civic onto a connecting road, she mentally outlined her article. It had been years since she fleshed out a story and the exercise was not pleasant, but necessary. It gave her structure. And it kept her thoughts focused on the task at hand, preventing her mind from wandering and, in this case, wallowing in grief for the other murder victim. Jimmy Mullins.

In all her thirty-two years on earth, seven of which she spent covering crime for the *Beacon*, Kara had never been exposed to any murders. Now there were two. And as she allowed herself to indulge in asking "Why?", an impossible question to answer in at least Jimmy's case, she nearly forgot she was driving.

The sight of a huge orange Home Depot sign in the distance shook her up. She'd driven several miles in a haze and now she was jerked back into reality. Earth to Kara. She needed packing boxes, and bubble wrap. Enough to pack up her parents' house.

Kara hated shopping. Rather, she didn't mind shopping when she had money to spend. But buying large brown packing boxes and reams of bubble wrap was not her idea of a good time. Grabbing an orange push cart that veered to the right, Kara defied the pushcart with a mind of its own and made it through the aisles of past paint cans and floor tiles, nails and tall rolls of carpeting until she found what she came for. She pulled several groupings of folded boxes off the shelf, found the bubble wrap nearby and made her way to the front of the store to check out.

It was all so mundane. And yet it really wasn't. And that's when the gravity of what she was doing, preparing to pack up her parents' past as well as her own, overcame her. And there, in the checkout line of the Home Depot, amidst the stubby men in their grubby jeans and T-shirts, their rough hands and heavy accents, Kara started to cry.

She was crying for herself, for her loss. The loss not just of her mother, and the loss of the Pa she used to know, but for Jimmy Mullins and the warm memories of her youth. And the way he died, senselessly murdered, was new territory for her raw emotions.

The woman at the checkout returned her credit card and stared into Kara's blubbering eyes. She wanted to blurt out "life isn't fair!" but what good would it do? So she willed herself to push the orange cart back out to the parking lot, get into the privacy of her car, and indulge in a good cry.

Chapter Eight

No sooner had Kara returned home when she was greeted with a loud "meow" from her new furry friend. And, for a moment, she forgot her sadness.

"Hey, didn't I just feed you?" Kara bent down allowing the tiny creature to rub against her hand as she opened a can of food. "Is this your brunch? Lunch?" She wasn't sure. Little Grey always seemed to be hungry. Kara spooned the contents onto a plate while Little Grey nosed at the spoon, an attempt to hasten things along. Kara watched as she gobbled it up. Kara could have stayed there, watching, lost in the innocence of a tiny, helpless animal who offered her nothing more than love. But she couldn't. She had work to do. A first draft. She needed to get to work.

Jumping back into writing was not going to be easy. Writing anything that had to pass Jack Logan's approval was a challenge, an exercise that was part creative writing with the focus on all the positive aspects of Nancy Harding's life at Twin Oaks, and part investigative reporting, a tip-toe around the notion that Nancy's death from arsenic came in the form of her weakness for cupcakes. To please Mrs. Warren, Detective Cirelli and skirt a defamation lawsuit for the Beacon, the story couldn't point the finger at anyone in particular. To please Jack Logan, her story had to raise doubts, to insinuate that Ricky Wexner was the likely culprit, without saying as much.

It took Kara three hours to get the right tone. She reread the piece one more time, then was ready to email it to Mrs. Warren for her review. But as she was about to hit the "send" button, she was distracted by the sound of hammering coming from Joe Collins' house.

A quick glance through the patio door made her smile. It was Joe all right. He appeared to be repairing a section of the shed, the one his mother had built for the feral cats. Kara watched as he finished securing part of the roof, hammering boards back into place. Then he moved a cluster of bright yellow mums in their terracotta pots and placed them to form a sort of "path" leading to the shed.. The bright flowers classed up the place for the "tenants." Kara smiled. She was starting to really like this guy … very much. But in the next moment, she chided herself for feeling so vulnerable. She hardly knew Joe Collins. He seemed nice enough, but she had to be careful. Her heart was in a tender place. "I hardly know this guy.." she reminded herself, then returned to the laptop and sent the story off to Mrs. Warren for her approval. Now she had to wait for Mrs. Warren to read it and, hopefully, not make any significant changes.

Meanwhile, she had packing to do. Lots of packing. And using the "Swiss cheese method," where you poke holes in a large project by taking small bites out of the toughest part, she decided to start in her parents' bedroom. But before she even got near it, she heard her phone buzz. It was her realtor, Connie Belford.

"Hi, Doll! Good news! The Orientals want to close in thirty days."

"Thirty! Connie, I can wait sixty days." Sixty days was the deadline for when the last payment to Twin Oaks was due. And Kara needed every single day of that period to pack up an entire house. "I need more time."

"They sold their place and need to be out in thirty days. You should be happy, Kaa-ra."

Connie had her over a barrel again and knew it. She could do nothing else but agree, but already she could feel her heart palpitating with anxiety. How on earth was she going to get everything done in time? And more importantly, where was she herself going to live?

She hung up and wasted no time getting to work. Entering her parents' bedroom, she was greeted by the scent of her mother's cologne. No time to indulge in sentimentality. She got straight to the task at hand, unfolding and decreasing the first of the boxes. Then she braced herself as she went to her mother's dresser and opened the top drawer.

It was squared off by a pink plastic divider from what used to be called the "five and dime" but was now known as the "dollar Store." Handkerchiefs in one compartment, folded and scented. Costume jewelry … bracelets, earrings, bobby pins, broaches, rosary beads in the other. Along the longer, narrow side compartment, a pair of knitting needles. The scent of Jean Nate permeated everything. When her phone suddenly buzzed, she welcomed the emotional distraction. It was Jack sending a text with a link attached. A story from a few years back in some women's magazine about Ricky Wexner and his acting career. He was clearly pushing the "Wexner did it" angle.

Kara took a moment to scroll through the article. It was about a TV show that made Ricky Wexner an idol among the teeny bopper set. "Delphin Daze." She remembered it well and never missed an episode. Every day after school, especially in the fourth and fifth grades, Kara's ritual was the same. Drop off her books, grab a snack, and switch on the TV to watch Ricky Wexner as Lance Lerner swimming with his pet dolphin, Nipper. It was every kid's dream to be Lance. He never seemed to go to school, always lived in perfect weather, and cavorted daily with Nipper.

But the gist of this story was not about Ricky's acting career but about his drug problem, the fate of many child actors who reached puberty and were no longer cute and clever. Even in his early teens, Ricky was in and out of drug rehab centers. Kara did the mental math and realized that Ricky had to now be about forty. And apparently he was still battling drugs.

The article went on to talk about Ricky's parents dying tragically in a car crash and, had it not been for his "Aunt Nancy," he would have no relations.

Kara knew what Jack was doing. He was being Jack, pressing her to push the angle about Ricky Wexner's drug use and to infer that druggies will do anything for a fix … even commit murder.

She was about to call him back to defend her journalistic integrity when she saw his name pop up on her caller I.D.

"Fitz, where's my draft?"

"I'm putting the finishing touches on it right now," she lied.

"I need it asap. With the autopsy results ready, someone in the lab could leak it to one of the tabloids and there goes our front page. You get it?"

"I'm on it, Jack." She hung up and immediately called Mrs. Warren. Thankfully, she picked up immediately.

"Miss Fitzgerald, I was under the impression that your story would be a pleasant feature about the good life we provide our guests at Twin Oaks."

"But it is … "

"I'm disappointed that you mentioned the arsenic."

"But if I didn't, Mrs. Warren, another publication would. And they might even insinuate that someone on your staff was responsible. At least my story doesn't cast blame. It simply states the facts." Kara waited. She knew she was right. "Mrs. Warren, I have found that honesty is always the best policy. By admitting that Nancy's death was not natural, you will be getting in front of any bad publicity. I can also insert in my story how Twin Oaks is cooperating with the police to make sure that no other guest in your care will be harmed. It's a strategy that will work in your favor."

"I understand, Miss Fitzgerald, as long as you insert a reference to how long most of my staff has been with me … decades … and that I implicitly trust each and every one of them."

"Of course. I can also add a postscript that my own father is one of your guests."

"Good. And please add a paragraph that I don't believe Ricky Wexner had anything to do with his aunt's murder."

Kara paused. It had been clear to her when they first spoke that Mrs. Warren didn't like or trust Ricky Warren, especially since he was bringing cupcakes to his diabetic aunt. Why now did she need to say that she thought he was innocent? It would be better for her not to say anything about him in the article. "If you believe he is innocent, then who do you think sent those cupcakes after Ricky left town? I plan to speak to whoever took the order at Vitale's bakery."

"Are you inferring that Ricky Wexner had an accomplice? That he charged someone with sending the cupcakes after he was back in Florida and had them insert arsenic into them?"

"I would never accuse anyone of a crime. That is for the police to do. But you have to admit it is strange that the very same cupcakes arrived after Ricky left town. It's a possibility he had an accomplice. I think it's my job as a responsible journalist to raise legitimate questions. I wouldn't attribute the question to you, of course."

"Well I'm sure the police will sort it all out. My only desire is that Twin Oaks be portrayed as the caring, warm and secure home away from home that it is."

"I agree. After all, if I didn't believe those things, I wouldn't have put my father in your care."

Mrs. Warren reluctantly agreed to the piece. Kara held back the fact that there might be another story, that there might even be a "series" of articles that covered the crime as more facts unfolded. But, like the Swiss cheese method, she was taking one bite at a time. She'd tell Mrs. Warren after the first story appeared in tomorrow morning's edition.

With the minor changes they agreed to, Kara reviewed the piece one last time then sent it off to Jack Logan. As he was under a deadline to get it to press quickly, she hoped he'd limit his edits and stick to the spirit of the piece so she wouldn't have to make excuses to Mrs. Warren for veering too far off their agreed to course. Now it was time for a cup of tea. And a chance to exhale. Once that story appeared tomorrow morning, she would be paid. It wouldn't be a lot, as it was only one assignment, but it would be enough to pay bills and buy some food, including some cat food.

Chapter Nine

Kara had filled an entire box with memories of her mother. She pushed past her watering eyes and started to pack up a second box when she stopped. She could continue the painful task later. But now she needed a distraction. That distraction was her second story. The story about who left the tainted box of cupcakes. Then, as if reading her mind, Jack called.

"Did you talk with Vitale's? Find out who ordered those cupcakes after Wexner left town? Who paid for them? Who picked up the box?: it was paid for and who picked it up."

Kara was emotionally drained. She was planning to rest, to sit on the patio with a cup of tea and distract herself from packing and writing and … crime.

"Jack, I planned to follow up on that tomorrow. For the second story. But I'm sure the police know already. Did you contact Detective Cirelli?"

"I think I'm on his shit list."

"Why? What did you do?"

"It's what I didn't do. I think. His wife invited me to supper a few Saturday's ago and I said I'd come but never showed."

"Why not?"

"I don't know. Got busy, I guess." Kara knew he was lying. Jack Logan was never busy. In fact, he was the only person she knew who went bowling alone. He was a true loner, and seemed to like it that way.

"Well you have to apologize. Send Mrs. Cirelli flowers with a nice note."

He hesitated. "I hate doin' that stuff. I'm not good at it."

"Nobody's good at saying they're sorry. That doesn't mean you shouldn't do it."

He was silent. "Just talk to someone at Vitale's. If tomorrow's edition sells well, I'll need your second installment by end of day. I think I can stretch this into a series."

"And your publisher will be happy." She wanted to add, "And then I'll get paid" but she decided to leave well enough alone. She was happy to be back to writing for the *Beacon*.

"And I'll have a reason to ask him to put you back on staff," Jack said, knowing what she had been thinking. Kara knew he was holding out a carrot. Telling her, without actually saying it, that she could have her old job back IF she delivered. And delivering meant writing stories that moved the *Beacon* off the newsstand.

Kara got the message loud and clear. She tossed a brush through her hair and fixed her lipstick. She was on her way to Vitale's bakery.

The woman who took the order from Ricky Wexner was actually from the Vitale family. A chubby, middle-aged blonde with clear brown eyes and a mouth that drooped downward. "I already told the police everything."

"The order came through a burner phone?"

"Yeah. They told Johnny, that's the kid who works here after school, to charge the cupcakes to Ricky Wexner's credit card. We had it on file from when he was picking up cupcakes every day for his aunt."

"Did Johnny recognize Wexner's voice?"

"The police asked him the same thing. He said he didn't. But it was a man. He just said send the same cupcakes and leave them outside."

"Outside?"

"Yeah. We leave day old bread out in front of the store after closing. For homeless folks and for the local shelter. Someone from there picks it up, usually around midnight. Whoever Johnny spoke to must have known that we do this, leave the bread outside because they said leave the cupcakes out there to be picked up. So we did. Thinking it was odd but Wexner is an odd duck."

"Do you have security camera in front?"

"No. There's a street camera but it doesn't get a view of the sidewalk. Just our front door."

Kara didn't have a lot of information, but enough to write a second story, and there would certainly be a third. Whoever called Vitale's knew about the bakery's habit of leaving bread out in front after closing. Someone who, perhaps, worked at the bakery or knew someone who did. Or someone who worked at the homeless shelter that picked up the bread. Was that person Wexner's accomplice? Or someone else who wanted to make it look like Wexner was involved?

Chapter Ten

"Jack, I've got enough to write a story about how someone placed an order for the cupcakes using Wexner's account at Vitale's. It came from a burner phone. I don't want to point the finger, but it's looking more and more like Wexner. I mean, who else would stand to benefit from Nancy Harding's death?" Then Kara answered her own question. "Nancy threatened to take Wexner out of her will if he didn't go to rehab. By all accounts, he's got no money of his own. But someone else could be framing him? Who else is mentioned in Nancy's will? Maybe someone who works at Twin Oaks? "

Jack was quiet, a rarity for him, then: "Find out if Harding was close to anyone at Twin Oaks. Get me a draft asap. I'll put it in tomorrow's edition."

Kara was about to hang up, to start writing, when she asked off-handedly, "Did you apologize to Mrs. Cirelli?"

"Yeah," he said it in a tone that could be confused with someone admitting to eating fried locusts. "And?"

"I got Cirelli himself on the phone."

"Oh … good. I'm sure he appreciated your apology to his wife."

"I guess. Asked him about the Mullins case."

"And?"

"Nothing. He said we can't do anything until the Archdiocese gives the go-ahead for the police to ask the public for help." Then: "But the autopsy's done."

"Already?'

"Fast tracked it for the parents' sake."

"That means the Mullins can have a wake and a funeral."

"Yeah. A wake without any people."

"Well if you find out where the wake will be ..."

"Uh ..." he hesitated.

"Jack? Do you know when it will be?"

"It's today. Cirelli said it's at Higgins funeral home. You know it?"

"Yes."

"Four o'clock till I guess closing."

"Four o'clock? I'd better get myself ready."

"You know you still can't write anything, Fitz. Not yet."

"I know. I just want to go to pay my respects. If only so Jimmy's parents won't be there alone."

Chapter Eleven

Kara hung up and checked her phone for the time. She had exactly two hours to shower, dress and get to the funeral home if she wanted to be there when the Mullins' arrived. Though she vaguely knew Jimmy's parents, only from seeing them around town now and then, she couldn't imagine how they would feel to be there alone, looking into a casket at their dead son. And with the Archdiocese keeping the news about Jimmy under wraps, that's exactly how it would be. An empty wake. That's why Kara was determined not to let them go through that kind of grief on their own. Nobody should face what they were facing without support.

She was about to go upstairs to get ready when the doorbell rang. She was annoyed. It could only be Connie Belford. Only Connie would come unannounced, as if the world was always at the ready for her arrival. Instead, Kara opened the door to see a smart, sophisticated woman about her own age. She was dressed entirely in black. Even her sunglasses had black rims.

"Can I help you?"

She tried not to stare at the woman's hair. It was a pretty but unnatural shade of soft copper with subtle highlights, surely an expensive coloring job. Her makeup was flawless, a masterful painting of tints against a peaches and cream canvas. The woman oozed money.

"Kara?"

Kara had no idea who this woman was, and why she knew her name. "I'm sorry, I ..."

"It's me! Sue Billings." She stopped. "I mean Sue Butler. Billings is ... soon to be *was* ... my marriage name."

A hornet's nest of memories from high school pricked at Kara's brain. Sue Butler was a member in good standing of the Nelligan Catholic clique. In other words, the mean girls' club. Never a friend to Kara or anyone who she didn't consider "cool." or worthy of her indulgence, Sue was one of those girls who looked, even in high school, like a woman. Attractive, smart and cunning, she was the ultimate social climber. Clearly she had finessed the art and done well for herself. A shiny bronze Mercedes was parked in the background. Now Kara could only wonder what the heck, after all these years, was Sue Butler doing here?

"Sue! Yes!" Kara tried to be polite. It was how she was raised. "Be gracious," her mother would always say, "to everyone." But that was easier said than done, especially with the memory still fresh in her mind of how Sue Butler could be downright cruel to those she felt were beneath her aspired status … namely the pimpled, the shy or the scholastically struggling.

"May I come in?"

Kara was uncomfortable and about to answer "this isn't a good time" but was side-tracked when Little Grey started rubbing against Sue's boot. She always heard that an animal's instincts about people were usually correct, and that any girl dating a man for the first time should put him through the "pet test" by exposing her dog or kitty to the guy to see if the animal took to him. It the guy passed the pet test, he was a keeper. Little Grey clearly "took" to Sue, so Kara invited her in, and wondered if, maybe, Sue Butler, now Billings, had changed.

"I'm sorry about the fur on your boots. She's a stray but she's very friendly."

"No, it's okay." She bent down to stroke the little cat. "I like animals." This was clearly a "new Sue".

"Can I get you some tea?"

"Thanks. But I can only stay a little while. I saw the For Sale sign and wondered if you still lived here. I always liked this house."

Kara couldn't imagine what Sue Butler, even a revised version of her, would find appealing about a basic Cape Cod. Still, everything about this new version of Sue seemed better, nicer, more mature.

"I actually just sold it." Kara smiled. "Now all I have to do is find a new place to live."

Sue looked at her curiously. "Yes. Well ..." she removed her sunglasses. Her eyes were watery. "I don't know if you heard ..."

"You mean about Jimmy Mullins ..."

Sue exhaled in relief. "Yes! Oh, I had to talk to someone who'd understand." Kara wondered how she had suddenly become one of Sue's confidants when throughout high school she was lucky to get a sideways glance from the girl. "You know Jimmy became a priest."

"I heard that." Kara motioned to the kitchen. "I just put the kettle on. Let's talk in there." Sue nodded, then helped herself to a seat at the kitchen table. "Milk and sugar?"

"Just milk. Thanks." Sue glanced around the room, the way people do when they have something to say but are summoning up the words. Then ... "A group of us from Nelligan ... we all went up to the Hague mansion last weekend for a three-day retreat. Jimmy was trying to help us repair our marriages."

"A group from Nelligan?"

"Yes. Regina Salvati and her husband Ray. I forget her marriage name. Me and my soon-to-be-ex, Steve Billings. You wouldn't know him. We met in college. And Cindy Summerfield and her husband, Dennis Gregson. He's an accountant and, well ... Jimmy was there as sort of our therapist and friend. He said mass every day for us, heard our confessions and there was some group therapy. It was good ... for the others. But it wasn't enough to save my miserable marriage."

"I'm sorry."

"No, don't be. I'm just glad I learned the truth before we had children. Anyway ... " her voice trailed off. It was an awkward moment until Kara broke in.

"Sue, I must say I'm surprised that Cindy and Jimmy never married. They were the big couple at Nelligan. Everyone thought they were made for each other," Kara added, though in truth, Kara spent a great deal of time on her knees back in high school praying that Jimmy would wake up one day, see the light, and dump Cindy for her.

"I know. Cindy never told me why, but they broke up after we left Nelligan. She met Dennis her freshman year at college and that was that." Then Sue added, "Jimmy was too good for her." Kara was surprised to hear Sue being so transparent, especially about a so-called "friend.".

"Jimmy broke up with Cindy?" Kara couldn't imagine any woman in her right mind throwing over someone like Jimmy Mullins.

"No, no. It was Cindy who broke up with Jimmy." She paused. "Between us, I think Cindy wanted someone with more of a future. I mean, Jimmy is ... *was* a hard worker. He drove a truck for a while and took online college courses. Finally got his degree ... but he never had ambition, I mean ambition to make money. He wasn't cut out to make a lot of money and Cindy wanted that."

Sue took a sip of tea then stared at the old cabinets and countertops. No granite or stainless steel here. Just old-fashioned simplicity.

"This is a very comfortable kitchen."

"Thank you."

"I hope I'm not keeping you from anything."

"No, It's fine. I was just about to get ready for Jimmy's wake."

"That's where I'm headed." Sue took another sip. "You heard he was stabbed." Sue paused. "Did you know he spent most of his time ministering to street gangs?" Her tone was accusatory.

"But wouldn't a gang member stand out at the Hague mansion? And if Jimmy was helping them, why would they want him killed?"

"I don't know why. Some people are just plain evil. You've been to the Hague mansion. It's surrounded by woods." She took another sip, her eyes darting to a loose flap in the wallpaper, something Kara forgot was there. "The police are talking to all of us who were on the retreat. They asked us to think hard if we saw anything ... anyone suspicious. I told them my suspicions about the gang members ..."

"But you never saw someone who looked like a gang member there."

"No ... but those guys are sneaky."

"But you didn't see anyone."

"No ... then again, I left the retreat the night before the others. I couldn't stay another minute and listen to Steve blurt out lies about our marriage. Anyway, enough about him." Another sip. Her peach lipstick was all over the rim of the once pristine cup. "I just needed to talk to someone from Nelligan ... who knew Jimmy back then. You know. The boy we all loved. When we were all kids and life was simpler."

"I understand. And I'm glad others who knew Jimmy will be at the wake. I was afraid I'd be the only one."

"Oh, no. I checked in with Jimmy's parents. They told me and I got out the word."

Kara nodded. "Sue, like you, Jimmy was a friend to me as well."

"I know. What's why I knew I could speak with you. I mean, I was there. Those gang members could have been hiding in the brush. Have you been to the grounds of the Hague mansion? Jimmy was killed on one of the hiking paths. They could have been lying in wait for him. We all walked those paths to clear our heads."

"Are the police talking to them? The gang members?"

"I don't know. I'd think they should."

"And what about the person who found Jimmy?"

"It was a group. From some bank. They checked in after us. You see, our retreat was over the evening before. Jimmy was found the following morning. Mid-morning, I believe the police said."

"So none of you were around when Jimmy's body was found?"

"Some might have been lingering … packing up. I personally left. Like I said, I got out of there. Drove back the evening before, after dinner. But at the dinner Jimmy did mention that he was gonna take a hike early the next morning and asked if anyone wanted to join him. I said at the time that I might, but changed my mind. Nobody else took him up on it. We were all spent.." She held back a spray of tears. "I wish I had gone with him. He'd be alive today."

"No, no, you can't think that way, Sue. You might have been murdered yourself."

Sue wiped her eyes with a handkerchief, but her mascara was already smeared from tears. "What time will you be at the wake?"

"Uh, I was hoping to get there early. When the viewing started. Four?"

"I figured you'd be there early. For private time with him. What with your relationship to Jimmy and all." Kara was taken off guard by Sue's last words. *Relationship*? Sure, Jimmy had come to her rescue a few times and always treated her nicely, as he did with everyone at Nelligan, but it was no relationship. It was barely an acquaintanceship.

"If you don't mind, could I meet you there? At four? Out in the parking lot? I don't want to go with my ... with Steve. I'd prefer to get there before he arrives, before he gets out of work."

"Sure. That would be fine."

They finished the tea. It was cold by now anyway and the conversation seemed to be over. Kara walked Sue to the door, past a stack of packing boxes.

"When are you moving?"

"I have to close in thirty days. Hopefully by then I'll be able to find an affordable place to stay." Kara laughed it off but it was a laugh underpinned by the stress she was feeling. Rents, she was learning, were through the roof. And she still didn't have a full time job. No landlord was about to take a chance on someone who wasn't currently working.

"You haven't found a place yet?"

"I'm looking. So if you hear of anything ... preferably cheap ... " she chuckled.

"I only ask because I may be able to help. I have a little cottage on my property. It's actually quite nice. Private. Built for household servants but my maid Maria prefers to live in the main house. We've been using it for guests. But if it goes unoccupied, Steve, my ex, well, he might get the idea to move himself in. I can't have that. Would you like it?"

"Uh ..." she couldn't answer fast enough. It didn't matter what the place looked like. She needed a home. "Yes. Sure. That would be great." Then she came to her senses. "Oh, I didn't ask about the rent."

"No rent. I insist. You'd be doing me a favor. Like I said, I don't want Steve to move in. That would defeat the purpose of the divorce. And the sooner I separate from him the better."

Kara had no idea what Steve had done to warrant the heave-ho, but she surmised it must have been pretty bad.

"Sue, I'd insist on paying you *something*."

"You can give me a hundred dollars a month. That work for you?"

"So little?"

"I don't need the money, but if you give me a hundred dollars, I can tell Steve that I have a paying tenant." She smiled. "So he wouldn't be able to kick you out. Now ... the cottage is on the far end of town. My home is in the Country Estates area." Kara knew the location by word of mouth. It was known for its "gentleman farmers," multi-millionaire Wall Street wonders, the modern day landed gentry with their acres of fertile soil, backyard golf courses, Tesla's and horse stables. But for Kara, the best part about moving to the Country Estates was that it was much closer to Twin Oaks. She could visit Pa twice a day. Sue handed her a card with the address and a sketch of a lovely mansion surrounded by rolling hills.

"So, is it a deal?" She extended her hand. They shook.

"Deal!"

Chapter Twelve

Bridget Cirelli had been counting the days till she got her husband back after thirty-five years on the force. She even booked them a cruise to celebrate his retirement ... a vacation she now had to reschedule. In all his years as a cop, and then as a detective, Pat Cirelli had never been faced with a single murder. Now there were two. The Nancy Harding autopsy clearly showed that the faded Hollywood star was poisoned and poor Father Mullins, well, that murder really threw her Pat for a loop. It was brutal and senseless. It had her hubby up at dawn and out the door before she even got a chance to wish him as much as a "have a good day." Now her inner gut told her what all cops' wives learn after vicariously spending decades on the force. That murders don't get solved overnight. It was going to be a long haul. And she had to buckle up in the passenger's seat for the bumpy ride.

After packing her man a turkey sandwich and a thermos of good coffee, (to replace the "gut rot" they served at the precinct), Bridget Cirelli set off. If she didn't bring Pat his lunch, he'd forget to eat. Or worse, he'd pop over to the vending machine and subsist on bags of pretzels and cans of soda.

After making her customary hellos around the precinct, Bridget entered a familiar office, only today it was messier than usual ... if that was possible ... and found her hubby deep in thought, hunched over a desk that looked like a hurricane's wake. A cone shaped lamp illuminated sheets of notes on yellow legal paper.

"I made you some fresh coffee. That stuff you guys keep in the pot's been there since Washington crossed the Delaware."

"Washington preferred tea," he smiled as he looked up from his paperwork. Then he opened the thermos, inhaled the aroma of fresh brewed coffee and smiled.

"You're a good wife, Bridget. I don't care what they say," he teased.

They shared a quick parting kiss, then Cirelli got back to work on both cases. On the Harding front, he had his guys checking out the nephew down in Boca. The "kid," who was actually near forty. Wexner was ensconced at the Riviera Rancho Recovery Center, a fancy name with an expensive price tag for rich people with addictions. So far, Wexner was the only person who stood to benefit from Nancy Harding's death. He was her only relative. At least the only relative that she acknowledged, not counting Nancy's three ex-husbands who were all dead. Still, Cirelli needed to get his hands on the will. To find out just how much Wexner stood to gain, or if there were charities and others who would benefit from Nancy's untimely demise.

But as much as Cirelli wanted to pin the murder on Wexner, there was the issue of the cupcakes being delivered after Ricky left town. Did he have an accomplice in crime? Who slipped the arsenic into the cupcakes? Was it someone who works at Twin Oaks? Or another "guest" who disliked Nancy's entitled attitude and decided she'd be better off dead. Cirelli couldn't rule anything or anyone out. Neither case was going to be a slam dunk. .

After a few bites of his turkey sandwich, Cirelli put the Harding folder aside and opened the file on Father Mullins. This one was particularly disturbing on several levels. For one, Cirelli was Catholic. He also knew of the young priest as he was a "local boy," growing up in Cirelli's own parish and attending the nearby Catholic high school, Nelligan. Father Mullins was known to be a very good man. Selfless. He was working in a poor parish, helping kids who had fallen in with gangs get back on track. Plus, there was no motive. No money to be gained. No jealous lover. For such a violent murder, with such ferocious stab wounds in the back, the killer was sending a message, making it personal. Not like Nancy Harding's poisoning where there was distance between murderer and victim. To the contrary, whoever killed this poor priest was full of hate and rage.

Cirelli pulled out the notes his guys took from a groundskeeper at the Hague mansion. One of the first interviews Cirelli got when he arrived at the scene was with a groundskeeper at the Hague mansion. The man said he saw Father Mullins that morning, in the front foyer, dressed in jogging clothes. They exchanged "good mornings" then Father Mullins did a few stretches before setting out on the trail. Alone. It was just before dawn.

The other interviews were with the people who attended the retreat. All except Sue Billings who had left the night before. This group of five were considered persons of interest, but none had any reason to fiercely stab a beloved priest. In fact the women, who all went to high school with Mullins, clearly adored him. The men thought he was a "good guy" and a "regular man's man," the words they used to describe the caring priest.

Cirelli carefully went over each interview as he sipped Bridget's coffee. Each couple came to the Hague mansion to fix their troubled marriages. If Father Mullins still got the ladies' hearts fluttering, could a jealous husband have taken revenge on the handsome priest? After all, one of the women, Cindy Summerfield Gregson, went steady with Mullins throughout high school. Did she harbor a crush on her former flame? Or was her hubby envious of their past relationship? Mullins not only had movie star looks, he was also known to be charismatic. Even the females on the force were gushing when they saw pictures of the guy. Could it be that one of the husbands, already on thin ice in his marriage, let jealousy consume him with rage and he simply snapped?

Cirelli looked up from his notes to stretch his neck, then poured the last of the coffee from the thermos into his favorite mug, one that his kids gave him years ago on Father's Day. It said, "World's Best Dad" on one side with an old photograph of him on the other ... a photo taken before he went on Weight Watchers ten years ago. That picture reminded him to stay on his diet. And if it wasn't his once chubby "mug" on the mug, it was his Bridget.

How he loved her and their four kids ... who were now all adults and living on their own. Soon there would be grandkids. But as much as he always tried to be there for his family, he gave up a lot, missing their sports games and school concerts, to do his job. He showed his love for his loved ones through his work, by keeping his community a safe place to live for his family and other families. Now he felt, at the end of his career, that he couldn't drop the ball. He couldn't retire until both these cases were solved and until those who committed these murders were behind bars for a long, long time.

Setting his coffee down, he returned his attention to the Harding folder. This case was the easier one to stomach as Nancy Harding, though certainly not deserving of being murdered, had lived a rich and full life for a lot longer than Father Mullins. And her death, while still tragic, wasn't as blatantly violent as being stabbed in the back eight times.

Earlier, he had seen something in Harding's file that stuck in the back of his mind. Something he thought he might need later ... something apparent but not obvious. Then his eyes fell on it. An interview with a staffer at Twin Oaks. A valet slash orderly named Daniel. He said that he noticed Nancy was recently talking about regrets in her life. That when he pressed her to tell him about it, she demurred. But Daniel said he sensed that something was troubling her, something from her past. Daniel said he was so concerned that he put her on suicide watch for a while. Cirelli found it odd that Mrs. Warren, the director, never mentioned this to him when they spoke. Could this be a suicide instead of a murder? He wondered. The orderly added, "She once told me that she could have had a family but sent them away. When I asked her what she meant, she shut down. I never mentioned it again. But I got the feeling that she was full of regrets."

Cirelli wondered, what did Nancy mean that she could have had a family? Mrs. Warren and Daniel said in their interviews that Nancy's only family member was her nephew, Ricky Wexner. And she had only sent him to rehab ... she had not sent him away in the sense that she kicked him out of her life. So who else was in this "family" that Nancy sent away?

Besides, if Nancy *did* poison herself, then she had to get hold of the arsenic to do it. Then she'd have to enlist an accomplice to pick up the cupcakes from the front of Vitale's and leave them on the front stoop of Twin Oaks. It was a long, drawn out way of doing herself in ... if it was suicide ... which was becoming highly unlikely.

"Detective, we just got a call from someone who wants to take possession of Nancy Harding's body," one of the rookie detectives on the case interrupted.

"Who? The nephew?"

"No. Her accountant."

"Her accountant?! What's his role in all this?"

"He's also the executor of her estate."

"Tell him not yet. But find out from him who Nancy named in her will. Who her beneficiaries are."

"In other words, follow the money."

"Exactly."

"Well, for what it's worth, we already interviewed him. He was on the retreat."

"Who?!"

"Dennis Gregson. Tall, skinny guy. Glasses."

"He's the executor?!"

"Yep." The rookie knew what his boss was thinking. "I know. I'm already on it."

A buzz from Cirelli's phone reminded him of something he almost forgot. That Father Mullins' wake was at four p.m.. He had only a few minutes to splash water on his face and run a brush over his teeth.

While Cirelli wanted to pay his respects to the deceased and his parents, there was another reason why he wanted to get to the wake as soon as it began. He wanted to see everyone who showed up. While the Archdiocese still wasn't allowing any publicity about the murder, Cirelli knew that news of the popular priest's death would get out to those who knew him. He was that popular. And, along with his friends, there was a good chance that his enemy would show up as well. It was well known in law enforcement that offenders often returned to the scene of their crimes. Arsonists, burglars, and murderers got a sick thrill out of seeing the damage they wrought. Police books said it was a subconscious desire to get caught. Whatever the reason, Cirelli planned to be there to survey every single mourner. And if the killer *was* there, Cirelli was ready to sniff the bastard out of the crowd.

Chapter Thirteen

Kara checked the time on the dashboard. She'd arrive at the wake, according to the GPS, in ten minutes. And she was dreading it. She feared how she'd react when she saw her friend laid out in a casket.

At a traffic light, Kara checked her face in the rearview mirror. Some mascara had smudged under her eyes. She had concealer in her purse that she could apply when she got to Higgins. But she couldn't conceal the pain she was feeling in her heart.

She hurt for Jimmy, but she also hurt for herself. His death reminded her that life was fleeting. That youth wasn't a guarantee of a future old age.

The GPS lady interrupted. Higgins was near. "Make a left at the Brr-GAR King." Then she saw the slate grey stone building in the distance. Neat. Clean. Potted mums. It stood out in the otherwise older and less well kept neighborhood. Kara pulled into the parking lot, which was already filling to capacity. Word had gotten out, she thought. Despite the Archdiocese's command to keep things quiet.

The doors to the funeral home had not yet opened but a queue of mourners was waiting in the dull, muggy air … a fitting response from nature to the sad occasion. Kara looked around for Sue's bronze Mercedes but it wasn't there. Though it was nearly four o'clock, Sue was running late. More cars arrived. Then her phone buzzed.

"I'm stuck in traffic," Sue sounded agitated. "I think it might be another fifteen minutes."

"No worries," Kara assured her. "I'll wait in my car till you arrive."

"Thanks." Sue sounded relieved.

Kara watched from the Civic as more cars filled up the dwindling parking spots. There was an extraordinary turnout.

Growing up, Kara and Pa used to "people watch," a pastime that later developed her skills as a crime reporter. She caught herself doing just that as she watched the eclectic characters arriving by car and foot and even some on a dilapidated, graffiti covered church bus.

There were those from Jimmy's parish, St. Aloysius ... or "St. Al's" as it was affectionately called. Poor people with big hearts. Hard workers. Dressed in their best, which translated to a clean and pressed shirt with work pants for the men and flowery blouses and flounced skirts for the women.

They made a sharp contrast with the crowd who knew Jimmy from Nelligan. They were the "suits" ... the young men and women in polished business attire. The women wore their hair shiny and long, highlighted with expensive chemicals, their makeup understated but flawless. The men worked out regularly and combed their hair back. The distinction of class was overwhelmingly palpable. An eclectic conga line was waiting for Higgins to open its doors.

Kara took in the crowd and wondered if Jimmy's killer was among them. Then, breaking the solemnity of the moment, an old Ford, transformed into a "low rider," announced its arrival with a gust of exhaust and a grinding clarion call.

As the lot was now full, the low rider edged itself into a spot along the street. Out stepped a menagerie of scary-looking young men. Chains. Muscle shirts. Loose jeans. And tattoos on every part of their bodies. They had to be "Jimmy's guys," Kara thought. The ragtag, errant street toughs he walked among, who he ministered to ... who he trusted. Kara, as good a

Christian as she tried to be and knowledgeable of Jesus's admonition to "judge not lest you be judged" was judging them. And in her eyes, every one of them could have been the killer.

She observed the interplay among them. They were clearly out of their element, though they tried to camouflage their awkwardness with a united front. She watched, like people watch something they shouldn't be watching. And she had to admit, they were an engaging group, in their own way. Courtly in gestures as they cut the line but then held the doors open, allowing the elderly first, then ladies, then a man on crutches to enter Higgins in deserving order … deserving according to their own brand of justice. With the weak getting a pass. Surely none of them, with this chivalrous code of conduct, could take a charismatic priest's life? Or was this all a show to take the spotlight off of a dishonorable deed?

Kara checked the time. It was four-twenty. She wondered how much longer Sue would be. Then ... a soft blue BMW pulled into a space directly behind the gang members' jalopy ... a stark contrast.

The driver's door opened and a thin man in glasses with a bald spot got out first, then walked around to the passenger's side, opened it and outstepped someone Kara knew from the get-go. Cindy Summerfield. Jimmy's old flame.

The fourteen years since high school had been kind to Cindy … perhaps with a little help from Botox. Unfortunately, Cindy's husband looked rather worn down, a slip of a fellow who was playing the role of his glamorous wife's lapdog. He looked tragically weak. Kara studied the odd couple. While she was always taught that "looks aren't everything," Cindy was taking the old adage to the extreme in choosing to marry such a milquetoast man.

Reticent, submissive, those were two of the adjectives that sprang to mind as Kara studied the strange alliance. But one thing was for sure. The guy certainly checked the box when it came to being a good provider. Cindy was living in the lap of luxury, despite there being trouble in paradise. After all, wasn't why all the couples went on the retreat? Kara wondered if perhaps Cindy was still carrying a torch for Jimmy. Maybe her hubby sensed he had competition for his wife's love, flipped out and killed Jimmy in a fit of rage.

No sooner had Kara entertained the thought than she dismissed it. The guy just looked too weak for anything, much less stabbing a taller, buffer, more athletic man eight times in the back.

Kara watched as the Gregson's held hands while they entered the funeral home, Cindy taking a slight lead, Dennis trailing a few inches, keeping a wary glance on the gang members who were acting like a kind of "welcome wagon" at the door, directing the mourners inside as if they owned the place.

Kara glanced away from the entertaining spectacle to see Sue's Mercedes. She was backing into one of the last remaining spaces on the street. But left ample room for the black Chevy Bronco that pulled in behind her.

It was becoming a reunion of the Nelligan Mean Girls Club. Out of the Bronco stepped Regina Salvati, followed by her husband. The Bronco looked well worn, so did Regina who was already scolding her corpulent hubby about the way he parked. Another broken marriage that clearly wasn't mended on the ill-fated retreat.

Kara crossed the lot to greet Sue as she got out of the Mercedes, En route, she passed Regina and her hubby who were already arguing about something. "You okay?" Kara soothed.

Sue's eyes were puffy. She had been crying. "C'mon ... let's face this together," Kara said in a reassuring tone. Sue nodded and smiled weakly. As they reached the doors, they were greeted by a blast of air conditioned air, heavily scented with lilies, thick and heady on the muggy October day. With every wake she'd ever gone to, Kara grew less and less fond of lilies.

"I'm glad there's a crowd. Jimmy deserves a big send off." Kara's voice trailed off as they inched their way into the room where Jimmy was at rest. It was clogged with mourners. Person to person. She couldn't even see the casket.

His killer could be standing next to us, Kara thought. After signing the guest book, which was a ten minute wait until their turn came, she and Sue attempted to make headway against the human tide. For a death that nobody was supposed to know about, Kara thought, the turnout was extraordinary. And if the killer was in attendance, he or she could slip through the crowd unnoticed.

With persistence, and weak knees, they finally reached Jimmy's casket. Only a few tall men blocked their view. Then the tall tide parted and there he was. The Reverend James Patrick Mullins. Jimmy. Laid out in his Roman collar and black cassock. In other words, his "street clothes." The boy/man she never stopped loving from the time they met so many years ago. And she could only stare. Her legs weak. Her mind confused. Until she felt Sue's grip on her arm. Squeezing tightly.

"You okay?" Kara whispered. It was their turn to kneel at the casket.

"I need to fix my makeup," she said tersely, before she abruptly disappeared into the crowd, leaving Kara alone at the casket.

She wanted to run away too, but she couldn't. Wouldn't. It was hard, but Jimmy's parents were seated a few feet away and they deserved the respect of her attention. For their sake alone she had to stay, to kneel and say a "Hail Mary" while she stared into their son's lifeless, pale, face. A face that, though made up and mummified, still looked handsome. And kind. The face she was looking at for the very last time.

Suddenly she realized she was hogging the kneeler. There was a long line behind her. Kara pulled herself up from her knees and turned to face the Mullins. They looked frail. Gentle. Mrs. Mullins was standing. Mr. Mullins was in a chair, his head in his hands. Kara drew in a deep breath.

"Kara?" Mrs. Mullins said softly.

"Yes, Mrs. Mullins. I'm Kara Fitzgerald."

"I expected to see you here." Her next remark took Kara off guard. "Your dear mother and I used to chat almost daily about you and our Jimmy."

Kara thought Mrs. Mullins was confusing her with someone else. And who could blame her? With so many people sharing their "Jimmy stories," well meaning anecdotes about their son, it was sure to get confusing ... and draining. And while Kara never remembered her mother mentioning Mrs. Mullins, not as an acquaintance and certainly not as someone she spoke with every day, Mrs. Mullins' tone was confident.

"We'd meet at each other's houses for coffee. The two of you would be in the playpen together," Her eyes lit up at the memory. "You know how new mothers are. Nervous," she playfully squeezed Kara's arm as she smiled. "We'd compare who was the first to talk, or take a first step. Our Jimmy and you were always neck and neck ... walking, talking ..".

"I'm sure she enjoyed your company," Kara said, still believing Mrs. Mullins was confused.

"I was so sorry to hear she passed," she added soberly. Now Kara was beginning to wonder if there *was* a relationship between her mother and Mrs. Mullins, a long ago friendship that her mother simply forgot to mention. *Who else could Mrs. Mullins be talking about?* Still, if they had been friends, why didn't her mother ever mention the friendship?

The kind woman turned to her husband. The grief stricken man was staring at the floor. Kara's heart broke for him. He was lost. Mrs. Mullins returned her attention to Kara and smiled weakly.

"Jimmy always seemed to pop up whenever I needed help," Kara offered. "Thankfully, it wasn't that often," she softly chuckled. "But two times in particular he came to my rescue out of nowhere."

"That's because we told him to keep an eye on you."

"You did?" Kara was baffled. She wanted to follow up with *Why? Why would Jimmy need to keep an eye on me?* But she didn't. It wasn't the time or the place to ask. Beside, there was a growing line of mourners directly behind her.

"With both of you being adopted children ... well, I'm sure your parents felt the same way as Mr. Mullins and myself. That God chose us to be your *real* parents. That the young woman who gave you life was just that ... the person who brought you into the world. We took over from there. Jimmy was meant to be ours, and you were meant to belong to your parents."

Kara suddenly felt a soft hand on her arm. An older woman was moving her along. She was holding up the line.

Kara nodded, then kissed Mrs. Mullins on the cheek before shuffling through the crowd. She found a space to stand in the back. Sue was a few feet away, rapt in conversation with Cindy and Regina. Just like old times, Kara thought. The threesome that never included her.

An old priest arrived. Kara knew what this meant. He was here to say the rosary with the mourners. His face was ruddy. His gait quick, a "no nonsense" air about him, as if he trained prize fighters in another life. When he saw Detective Cirelli and Jack entering, the priest spun around to greet the detective. They exchanged a few words, the priest's voice loud and bellowing, the way stage actors speak, or those who emote from the pulpit … or the hard of hearing. Kara guessed it was the latter. Then the elderly priest moved through the crowd like a hot knife through butter and made a pronouncement that everyone should take a seat as he would be starting the prayers. Kara noticed a few people slip out. Others found a chair. The priest got right to it. Kara glanced over at Jack and Detective Cirelli who were sizing up the room. Observing every detail. One looking for a killer in their midst, the other for a good headline.

Sometime during the first decade, Kara gracefully moved toward the door, catching Jack's eye. He got the message and followed her into the foyer.

"So you and Detective Cirelli are talking again?"

"I apologized to his wife and that's that."

"And what does the detective think? Anyone here look suspicious?"

"Not yet."

"What did that old priest say to you too?"

"The one sayin' the rosary? He told Cirelli that Mullins was up for a promotion. To bishop. The youngest in the archdiocese. That's why the cops were asked to keep the investigation quiet."

"I don't understand. I thought they were afraid of copycats."

"They lied … according to that old guy, and I tend to believe him."

"What did he say?"

"That Mullins was likely rubbed out by another priest. That it was a conspiracy to get him out of the way to clear the path for others who were older and thought it was their turn to be bishop ... not some upstart."

"Some upstart!" Kara realized she'd raised her voice. She quickly composed herself. Others were listening. "So the archdiocese is protecting a murderer? Do you think the old guy …"

"His name is Father Dunleavy," Jack corrected.

"Do you think he's onto something or is he just a bit …"

"I don't know. Cirelli doesn't know. A priest killing another priest? It seems more likely that one of those guys with the tattoos did it."

"Yeah. Cirelli's checking them out."

Sue walked out of the room and caught Kara's eye.

"Kara? I'm leaving now. " She glanced at the door. "Dennis ... Cindy's husband ... he just told me that Steve is on his way. I don't want to run into him."

"Of course." Kara turned back to Jack. "Are you going to run a story? About jealous priests? You know it's only one man's opinion."

"Yeah, but it's a good story. Maybe as a sidebar. I'm thinking about it."

"Kara? Can I talk with you a second?" Sue called out. Kara left Jack and followed Sue to the parking lot. "You know you're welcome to move into my cottage any time. Like I said, I don't want to leave it empty for long. So the sooner the better."

"Thank you. I can't tell you what a load this is off my mind. And I'm very grateful. Would it be okay if I move in soon ... like within the next couple of weeks?"

"Make that days instead of weeks, okay? Like I said, I don't want my ... well, you know my reasons. I've gotta go now. He'll be here any minute."

"Thank you again, Sue."

Sue nodded then went to her Mercedes. Kara headed to her car. As she pressed the ignition, she watched Cindy and Regina crossing the parking lot toward Sue. They exchanged phony air kisses, a few words, then parted. Kara realized that Cindy and Regina had been waiting for her to leave Sue before they approached their old friend. *Still playing high school games*, she thought.

Sue drove off first. Regina and Cindy went to their respective cars where their husbands were waiting. Kara sat in her Civic as she watched the battered Bronco and then the powder blue BMW pull out. She could see through the BMW's rear windshield. Cindy was in the passenger's seat, raising a silver flask to her mouth. It took Kara off guard. Cindy Summerfield, the IT girl at Nelligan, married to an obviously successful man, needing alcohol to get through her old flame's wake. Kara wondered what Cindy's husband was thinking. *That he could never measure up to Jimmy Mullins? Perhaps. But, truth be told, no man could.*

Chapter Fourteen

It had been an emotional day. Kara drove several miles before she realized she had driven several miles. She would have kept driving in a mental fog if she hadn't met a speed bump. The sudden jolt to the car caused her purse to fall onto the floor. She had forgotten to zip it closed after removing her keys. Her wallet and phone fell out. Along with the holy card she picked up at the wake.

On one side was a lovely watercolor taken from a famous painting depicting the Virgin Mary ascending into heaven. Kara pulled the car over to collect it and everything else on the floor. That's when she turned the card over and saw what was on the other side.

It was a prayer. The Serenity Prayer of St. Francis. "God grant me the serenity to accept the things I cannot change, the courage to change the things I can, and the wisdom to know the difference." Beneath it in black Gothic typeface was "Reverend James Patrick Mullins" and the dates of Jimmy's birth and death. April 22, 1990 – October 14, 2022.

Kara did a double take. What were the chances that she and Jimmy were born on the same day?

Chapter Fifteen

She arrived home, greeted by a cascade of maple leaves that floated over from the house next door onto her driveway. Turning the key in the front door, Kara glanced around at all of the furniture, nick-nacks, pillows and throw rugs she'd need to pack up or ship out. Basically, it was all a reminder of "home."

She had to get tough with herself. "It's only stuff." That's what she told herself so she'd be able to set her emotions aside and pack it all up. It would be a good exercise. A chance to not think about how much it hurt her heart to sell her family home. Whatever she couldn't pack, like furniture and rugs, she'd donate. She presumed Sue's cottage was already furnished. But once she had a steady job and could afford her own place, she'd buy everything new. That would feel good, wouldn't it? she thought, trying to convince herself.

She set her purse on the Formica countertop in the kitchen, then filled the kettle to make tea. As she waited for the water to boil, she took out the holy card to make sure she really saw what she thought she saw.

Was it a coincidence? It could be. But it also made what Mrs. Mullins said at the wake make more sense … that she and her mother used to compare their babies' milestones. Still, why would she and Mr. Mullins ask Jimmy to keep an eye on her? What was that about?

As she poured the steaming water over the teabag, Little Grey strolled in from the living room and began to rub against her ankle. Kara realized she had forgotten to pick up cat food. And she was running out of the litter that Joe dropped off.

"I'm sorry. I'm not a very good mama. Give me time." Then she made her new friend a scrambled egg. There were only three left in the fridge. It was time to go to the market.

The egg was cooling when Kara heard a knock at the patio door. She knew it could only be …. Joe. And that made her smile. As if reading her mind, he was holding a palette of cat food.

"I picked up extra today at PetSmart. Maybe she'll like it," he nodded to Little Grey.

"Thank you. And I'm sure she will. Beggars can't be choosers, right?" She paused. "How much do I owe you?"

"Oh, no, no. I kind of feel guilty that she came over here."

"Don't. She's a great little friend. Please, come in." He nodded as he carried the large palette of small tin cans into the kitchen. "Can I get you some tea? That's about all I have at the moment."

"Sure." He sat at the table as Kara set the cups and milk down.

"Sugar?"

"Better not." Then he took in her dress … a smart charcoal grey Calvin Klein that she found on sale two years ago at TJ Maxx. "You look nice."

"I was at a wake. For someone I knew at Nelligan."

"Someone our age! Were they a good friend?"

"Kind of."

"I'm sorry. To die just when you're really starting to live. Was she sick?"

"He … he was murdered."

Kara watched as the blood drained out of Joe's face. "Murdered? That's ... wow ... that's unbelievable. Did they catch the person? The murderer?"

"Not yet."

The taint of Kara's news hung heavy in the air.

"You want to talk about it?"

"There isn't much to say. Except that he was a good person. A priest." She paused. "He wouldn't hurt a soul."

She poured the water into the tea cups while Joe filled the long silent void by petting Little Grey. Kara wanted more than anything to talk to someone, to share what she was going through, but she hardly knew this guy. And she hated feeling "needy." Then again, she *was* needy. Needy for a good friend. Someone she could trust. When Pa was around, even with his dementia, she always felt she had someone she could talk to ... even when he really wasn't paying attention. Now she felt totally alone.

"Hey," he suddenly blurted out, as if trying to raise the tone in the room. "I got a job today. My business partner and I are gonna be building the new annex at police headquarters."

"Police headquarters? Wow ... " Kara tried to sound enthused but her emotions were still stuck in neutral. "That's great."

"I was gonna have a little celebration. Nothing fancy. Just pizza and a bottle of merlot. My folks have a pretty good wine collection. Feel like joining me later?"

Kara wasn't in the mood to socialize, but Joe wasn't just anybody. She already felt like he was a friend. "Yes. I would." She paused. "And I also have something to celebrate."

"Really?"

"Yes. I found a new place to live today."

 "Oh ..." He was clearly disappointed. "Where?"

"It's only temporary. I need to sell this place to pay for my Pa's care. But this girl ... woman .... I knew at Nelligan ... well, she said I could stay in her guest house. It's in Country Estates."

"Country Estates?! Not too shabby. When will you be moving?" He was leaning down to pet Little Grey.

"She needs me to move in as soon as possible. But I'll have to pack up this place first."

They filled the air with small talk about the weather and cats and sipped tea. Joe inserted that he'd once been in the Navy. But the elephant in the room was that Joe didn't want her to move and she didn't want to either.

"Well ..." he stood to leave, taking his cup to the sink. "It's gonna be a nice evening. Indian Summer weather. How about I stop by with the pizza and wine in about ..." he checked the time on his phone "two hours?"

"Sounds like a plan."

As he walked off, through her yard and into his, Kara watched, and thought about how much she liked this guy. She liked him very much.

Chapter Sixteen

Pizza and wine under the stars with a kind, intelligent and handsome man on a comfortable autumn night. Kara thought it couldn't get much better than that. Best of all, Joe loved animals, a sign of good character.

They ate and laughed. Kara had brought out some shawls to ward off the evening chill. Joe found some firewood in his parents' garage and got a fire going in the pit that the Fitzgerald's used to use. It was all very comfortable, and natural.

They said goodnight about eleven with Joe kissing her on the cheek. Kara watched him cross through the adjoining yards and fade into the darkness. Lost for several minutes in happy thoughts, Kara almost didn't hear her phone buzz. It was Jack.

"Jack? It's eleven." She remembered that Jack was the kind of person who needed boundaries or he'd be phoning any time of the day or night. She swore he never slept.

"You got an outline on the second Harding story? About the arsenic?"

"Not yet ..." He took her off guard. "My first article didn't come out yet."

"It's in the morning edition. I'll need your second installment by noon."

"Okay, Jack. But I'd like to keep Mrs. Warren in the loop. The tone of this piece will be different from the first and if I don't show her the courtesy, I may lose access to her and her staff for future pieces."

"You know I don't like showin' drafts to anyone."

"I understand. But you also have to understand her point of view. It won't look good for Twin Oaks to say that one of their guests was allowed to be poisoned."

"We're puttin' the blame on the nephew, right? Shouldn't be a problem for Twin Oaks."

"Jack, the police haven't officially called Ricky Wexner a suspect. He's still only a person of interest. That's why our readers will assume that anyone, especially anyone working at Twin Oaks, could have done it."

"And what if that lady who runs Twin Oaks says she doesn't want us to print any more stories about Harding?"

"Jack, think this through. The *Beacon* can't afford a defamation lawsuit. Let me write something that suggests but doesn't accuse." She tried to sound firm. And while she didn't say it, her intention was to do as she originally planned … to show her draft first to Mrs. Warren to make sure she was on board with the story. It wasn't as much about getting her permission, but about staying in her good graces. With Pa now in her care, Kara couldn't afford to be on Mrs. Warren's bad side. Good night, Jack."

"Wait. That wake today … that was awful, wasn't it?"

"Seeing Jimmy in a casket? Yes. That was pretty awful."

"No. I mean that old priest …"

"Father Dunleavy?"

"Yeah. He really thought that the Archdiocese was clamping down on announcing Mullins' murder because they were protectin' one of their own."

"What did Detective Cirelli say? Does he believe the old man?"

"Well, Fitz, it's a mute point now."

"What do you mean?"

"Dunleavy's dead."

"Dead?!"

"Heart attack. Half an hour after he left Higgins. Barely got home when he bit the bullet."

"Oh, that's terrible. But he was old, and I'm sure he felt stressed … believing that Jimmy was killed by another priest."

"And who's to say that Dunleavy wasn't gettin' too close to the truth and got knocked off himself."

"Jack!"

"Fitz, think about it. Too much of a coincidence for my liking."

"So are the police investigating?"

"Cirelli's playin' it close to the vest. But if another priest killed Jimmy to get him out of the way from becomin' a bishop, then what would stop 'em from murderin' this old guy who was getting' too close to the truth."

"Are the police doing an autopsy?"

"Don't know. Like I said. He was old." He paused, then: "But the *Beacon* can get at the truth. Once Cirelli gets sick and tired of waitin' on the Archdiocese and we can start reportin' what the heck's goin' on."

Kara knew that Jack wanted nothing more than to scoop the online tabloids with a story about Father Dunleavy's conspiracy theory and subsequent death. She imagined he was already salivating at the idea of having a triumvirate of blockbuster news stories … Nancy Harding's demise, Jimmy's murder and Father Dunleavy's suspicions. All stories that lent themselves to big headlines that moved papers off the shelf and into the hands of readers.

There was only one hurdle. The online tabloids had a handle on young readers. That business model was attracting advertisers who wanted to reach the younger set … 18 – 34. The group that loved sensational headlines and innuendo and weren't as fussy about facts.

Jack detested this kind of so-called journalism. Kara thought he should have been born in another era, when newspaper men wore trench coats, felt fedoras, chain-smoked and camped out at the local courthouse to get the latest scoop.

"Jack, until the coroner rules the poor priest's death suspicious, we can't speculate." She gathered her thoughts. If she didn't rein him in, he'd spin out of control. "Let's first focus on Nancy Harding. We've got the edge on the tabloids. Let's keep goin' with that story, okay?." She drew in a breath. "I don't know about you, but it's very late and I'm ready to go to sleep. Good night, Jack."

Chapter Seventeen

But Kara couldn't sleep. She was restless and couldn't get settled. The only remedy was to get a jump on the next installment in the Nancy Harding saga. So she got up, took her laptop into the kitchen, and at one a.m. began to write. She wrote for a couple of hours, made several cups of tea in the process, and by four o'clock had a decent draft.

Would Mrs. Warren agree to this one? A story about the arsenic inserted into the cupcakes the killed Nancy Harding? Kara had to find out. After a quick read-through, she sent it off, then tried to get in a few winks before the sun came up.

Not much time passed when she was awakened by tiny paws touching her cheeks. "Breakfast time?" she groggily inquired of her powdery fur friend. Kara forced herself to her feet, wondering how she'd ever get through the day on only two hours of sleep.

Through the sheers on the front window, she spied a lovely ribbon of soft blue and pink on the horizon. The promise of a pleasant day. Her next order of business was to splash cold water on her face. That's when she heard the knock at the patio door and did a double take. Was it Joe? It seemed awfully early to call. It wasn't yet seven.

Tentatively, Kara moved to the side of the curtains and peeked through a crack. It was Jack.

"I tried the front door but your doorbell's broken."

"Jack, I worked all night. What do you want?"

Kara could see that Jack hadn't slept either. His eyes were bloodshot and his face needed a shave. Not to mention that his clothes looked as if they hadn't been changed in days. But that was Jack.

"Brought you this." He was holding out a Dunkin' Donuts bag in one hand and a cup of coffee in another.

"Oh..." It was out of character for Jack to do anything so thoughtful … for anyone … man, woman, child, dog, cat. And his gesture of kindness gave Kara pause. "Thank you."

"Well I was pickin' up donuts for the guys over at the precinct and thought I'd swing by and see how you were doin'."

"How am I doing? Oh, you mean … after Jimmy's wake."

"Uh, yeah."

"I suppose I'm as fine as anyone could be. It was sad. What about you? You okay?"

Jack looked down at his feet, the way people do when they are composing their next words. But the moment was interrupted when Kara looked off to see Joe coming through the yard, carrying something.

"Good morning!" she called out. Jack spun his head around, caught off guard.

"I found this extra litter box in the basement ... and another bag of litter. You should see the menagerie my mother keeps down there. Thought you could use it."

"Thank you! Joe, this is my editor ... Jack Logan. Jack, Joe's my neighbor. I adopted one of his ... well, his mother's stray cats."

Jack accepted Joe's handshake but it was clear to both Kara and Joe that Jack was miffed. Kara tried to soften Jack's prickly edge and smiled weakly at Joe, thanking him again, prattling on about how Little Grey was settling in nicely.

"Joe's been keeping us stocked with cat food and litter." She heard herself and knew she sounded stupid. Jack didn't care about cats or any pets. He might like them as a whole but they came just a tad above his tolerance for humans … which was pretty low.

"Well, I'll be going," Joe smiled. "Good meeting you, Jack." Jack's scowl remained in place as Joe walked off and then Jack, muttering, waved goodbye to Kara as he walked off too. Kara could only shake her head. She didn't dislike Jack Logan, but he was certainly a strange duck. And then a discomforting thought occurred to her. She'd always taken for granted that Jack was not interested in her or any woman. That his work was his first and only love. But seeing his reaction to Joe, like a jealous lover, made Kara wonder … and shudder. Could Jack Logan have a crush on her?

She shook the unsettling thought out of her head and went to take a shower. After dressing in jeans and a new shirt and cardigan, she was ready to see Pa at Twin Oaks. While there she'd stop by to see if Mrs. Warren had seen the second story. She sensed she'd have to do another "hard sell" to convince Mrs. Warren that coming clean about the arsenic was the only way to "get in front" of any negative publicity.

After a few bites of donut and a few sips of coffee, Kara checked the time. Visiting hours began at nine. It was now seven-thirty. She could use the time to pack. Her plan was to put all the boxes into storage until she found a new, permanent place to live.

Upstairs in her parents' room, she had one more dresser drawer to tackle. It contained her mother's nightgowns, most of which were outdated. But she couldn't just simply pitch them all in the trash. In a way, she felt it would be sacrilegious.

So, gently folding each one, Kara placed them in a box marked "donate." She was nearly finished with that drawer until she came to a manila folder. Its edges stuck to the base. Carefully, she pulled it out. Written on the tag, in her mother's perfect Palmer penmanship, was the word "Important."

Taking the folder downstairs to the kitchen, she would go through it later. But if anything inside was really that important, chances are it wasn't missed all these years. Then again, that word "important" piqued her curiosity. She took a look.

Chapter Eighteen

The top layer of documents was a menagerie of outdated receipts and certificates … records of oil changes and car repairs on cars her parents' no longer owned, her father's baptismal certificate, her parents' marriage license, and a plain bond envelope with a neatly folded letter inside.

And while the contents of the letter intrigued her, a quick glance at the time told her it was time to go. If she wanted to visit with Pa and also have time to catch Mrs. Warren before her busy day got underway, Kara knew she'd need to leave for Twin Oaks now.

On the way out, waiting on the front stoop in a bright yellow wrapper was the morning edition of the *Beacon*. The edition with her first Nancy Harding story. Pulling the plastic off, Kara unfolded the thin collection of paper to face the front page. Then she did a double take. Her story was relegated to a sidebar. And instead of the title she wrote, which was "Twin Oaks Takes Harding Death Hard," it was changed to "Harding Death Suspicious."

The main story with Jack's byline had the headline "Jealousy Kills Beloved Priest." *He's done it,* Kara thought. *He's gone too far and broken his promise to Detective Cirelli.*

Jack's story was everything he disliked about the tabloids. It was full of hearsay and speculation. Based on absolutely no facts but heavy on the late Father Dunleavy's unproven theory.

Kara could feel her stomach twisting into knots. Clearly Jack could no longer be trusted. First he wanted to point the finger at Ricky Wexner for Nancy's murder and now he's blaming some unknown priest in the Archdiocese for killing his rival, Jimmy, to get a bishop's mitre.

Chapter Nineteen

Kara's first impulse was to verbally wring Jack's neck. But then she settled down because she knew her anger and frustration wouldn't change anything. She could only concentrate of writing her own articles, staying close to the facts, and making sure to cross the t's and dot the i's. That is how she always tried to write.

She went back inside to toss the torn yellow plastic, still wet with dew, into the trash and her eyes fell on the curious envelope with the perfectly folded letter inside. Grabbing it off the kitchen counter, Kara took it with her.

When she got to the car, she was about to place the letter inside her purse to read later, but again, something, possibly the reporter in her, told her to take a look.

As the car warmed up, Kara unfolded the handwritten note on expensive bond. Unlike her mother's, this person's penmanship left much to be desired. It had the large rounded o's and a's and plenty of curly-q's that are usually found in young girls' diaries. It began "My dear children ..."

At first Kara thought that the "dear children" meant her parents. That this letter came from one of her grandparents, perhaps to the newly married Fitzgerald's. But as she read, she knew her first instinct was wrong. Particularly when she read the notation on a small notecard, same handwriting, that had been attached with a paper clip but was now separated, hiding in the envelope. It said, "please give this to them on their twenty-first birthdays." It was this last word, birth*days*, plural, that stymied Kara.

"My dear children,

I have asked that this letter be shared between your adoptive parents and given to each of you when you turn twenty-one.

I want you to know that there won't be a day that goes by when I don't think of you two. And I hope you, in return, think of me kindly.

I know you were both placed in good homes. Your parents may not have given birth to you, but they are kind and decent people who will take good care of you.

Perhaps some day we will meet. But until that time, I want you to know that I love you both dearly. That you are my proudest achievements. And that if I were a better person, a stronger person, I would keep you both. But I cannot. So I must keep you instead in my heart.

May you have wonderful, happy lives. And may you always know that you were conceived in great love.

Your birth mother,

Jane Jones

Kara held the letter in both hands and just stared. What was this all about? Who was this "Jane Jones" and, if she was her birth mother, then why had her mother never mentioned her. But even more puzzling was the salutation. "My dear children."

One question began to lead to another. Did her parents ever meet this Jane Jones? And, if they had, did they think it best that Kara not know about her? And, if Jane Jones was her real mother, then who was the other "child" she was referring to?

She was now full of questions, but with no one to answer them. She dared not ask Pa as he might not have been aware of the letter, or even have known about Jane Jones. And, after all these years, it would certainly confuse and even upset him.

After a second and then a third read-through, Kara pulled out her phone and did an online search of the name "Jane Jones." The only women with that name were either dead, much too old or much too young to be her birth mother. Or perhaps it was a pseudonym, a way to protect her privacy should she marry and have more children. Kara was confused, but determined. Whoever Jane Jones was, Kara was determined to find her.

Chapter Twenty

St. Aloysius was a tiny parish housed in a small brick building with a white-washed steeple, enormous bronze bell and tall, bold cross on top. The people who founded "St. Al's" in the late 1800s were Irish immigrants, poor, humble and full of faith. Now the parish was made up mostly of different nationalities, modest and faith-filled just the same, but from home countries with warmer climes. Clean and tidy, it was also struggling to make ends meet, and struggling to keep gangs with their cryptic messages in black spray paint from marring the facade.

It was Jimmy's funeral mass. The church was crowded with the have's and have nots … two worlds that Jimmy navigated. As a young man, he was part of the "haves." As a priest, well, he would give any of his parishioners the shirt off his back. These were very poor people. But decent. Kara could tell.

Like most funeral masses, this one was sad. It was difficult for Kara to focus. It wasn't the magnificent mahogany coffin in the center aisle, flowing with floral arrangements, that distracted her. It was the letter she read from Jane Jones. It had left her with a maze of questions. What was Jane Jones like? How old was she? And most importantly, were there really two babies and, if so, where and who was the other one? Somewhere out there in the world, Kara thought, she had a sister or a brother. And she desperately wanted to find them.

As the church got even more crowded and the funeral mass progressed, Kara scanned the crowd from her seat in the last pew. It was a mix, similar to the gathering at the wake yesterday but more so. An eclectic concentration of the struggling, hard working people, alongside the gang members with their chains and tattoos, their black leather and bald heads and, finally, the Nelligan crowd. The only person missing was Cindy Summerfield and her husband Dennis Gregson.

Kara caught a glimpse of Detective Cirelli and Jack Logan who had slipped into the church through a side door. The detective was scanning the crowd.

As Kara let it sink in that Jimmy, her dear friend, her hero Jimmy was only yards away in that polished wooden box, she felt her heart break. Literally break. It had only happened to her once before, when her mother died. But she recognized the sensation. It genuinely felt like a breaking of the heart. Her eyes full, tears began to slide down each cheek.

During the homily, the priest had kind words for the Mullins, who were seated in the front. Hee praised them as adoptive parents and lauded how their faith led their son to enter the seminary and become a priest. In fact, he said more about Jimmy's parents than he said about Jimmy himself. Kara thought that strange.

When it was time for communion, the Mullins rose from their seats first. Looking frail and tired, Kara wanted to give them both a hug. Clearly the magnitude of what had happened to their boy was taking its toll.

As the front pews emptied slowly, each communicant filing out into the main aisle to receive the Eucharist, some mourners touched the casket, some made the sign of the cross over it. Kara replayed in her mind what Mrs. Mullins told her yesterday. Could it really be? It was a long shot, but she had to know.

Chapter Twenty-one

After the funeral mass, cars processed to the cemetery. Kara followed and then, after prayers at the gravesite, lingered. Most of the mourners left, but Jimmy's parents remained, locked in grief, staring at their son's casket, which would not be lowered into the ground until after they left. Kara didn't want to intrude, and she decided not to insert herself into the Mullins' private moment unless they acknowledged her first.

"Kara, thank you for coming." Mrs. Mullins called to her.

"Of course." Kara walked over to the grieving parents.

"I hope you will come back to our house for coffee."

"I'd be honored. Thank you." Kara had the feeling that she was the only one from the funeral who was granted the invitation.

"We wish we could invite the others … but it would be too taxing." Then she smiled. "We're not as young as we used to be."

"None of us are," Kara heard herself reply. It was not the kind of thing she'd not normally say, but the past few days made her feel much older than she had even a week ago.

Kara started for her car. She planned to pick up a crumb cake from Vitale's bakery on her way to the Mullins. Then she spotted Detective Cirelli. And Jack. They were standing at a distance from the gravesite, engaged in a tense exchange. Kara could only guess what it was about. That Jack had basically derailed a police investigation by writing an article that not only announced Jimmy's murder, but pointed the finger squarely at some jealous, unnamed priest,

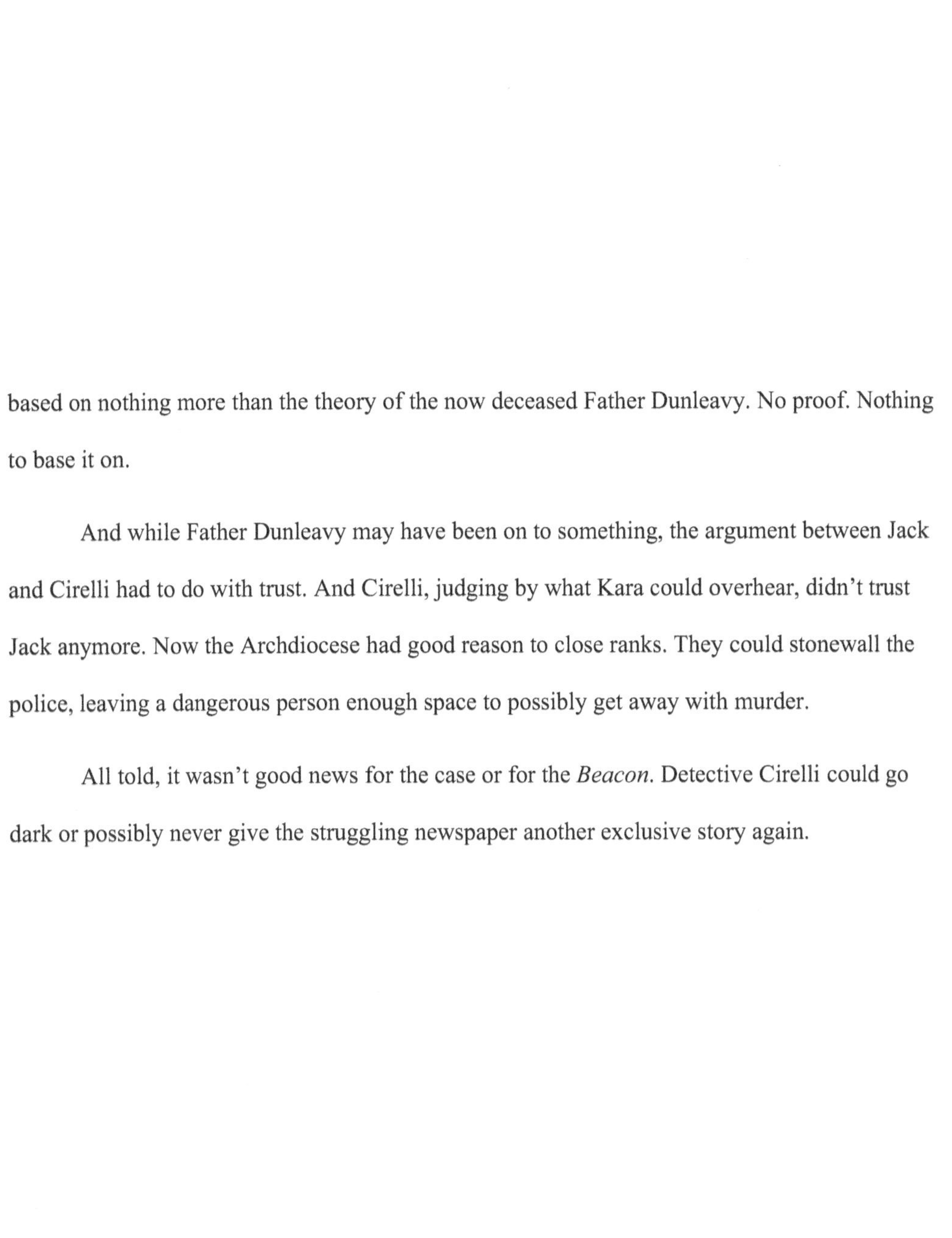

based on nothing more than the theory of the now deceased Father Dunleavy. No proof. Nothing to base it on.

And while Father Dunleavy may have been on to something, the argument between Jack and Cirelli had to do with trust. And Cirelli, judging by what Kara could overhear, didn't trust Jack anymore. Now the Archdiocese had good reason to close ranks. They could stonewall the police, leaving a dangerous person enough space to possibly get away with murder.

All told, it wasn't good news for the case or for the *Beacon*. Detective Cirelli could go dark or possibly never give the struggling newspaper another exclusive story again.

Chapter Twenty-two

As Kara pulled her Civic to the curb in front of the Mullins' modest home, she was surprised to see that their sedan wasn't yet in the driveway. Perhaps, she surmised, the remained at the gravesite a bit longer. While she waited in the car, her phone buzzed. It was Mrs. Warren.

"Hi, Mrs. Warren. Before you say anything, I want to say that I had to address the arsenic issue. As I explained, it's important to get in front of negative news and tell the Twin Oaks' side of the story first."

There was a hard silence. Then: "Kara, I'm calling about your father."

Kara felt her heart free fall into her stomach. "My father?! Is Pa okay?"

"He's fine." There was a pause, the way people pause when they're mentally selecting the proper words. "Someone left one of those bakery boxes at the entrance to Twin Oaks with your father's name on it."

"What?"

"It's fine. The police are checking the box for prints. The young detective I spoke with said it didn't appear as if the cupcakes were tainted." Kara knew by the descriptive "young" that it was not Detective Cirelli.

"Cupcakes! ... The same kind as the ones sent to Nancy Harding?"

"Yes." She paused. "Unfortunately, our security camera hasn't yet been fixed."

Kara felt her cheeks flush. Anger and frustration bubbling up. "Mrs. Warren, you told me ... never mind. As long as my Pa is fine."

"I promise you. I have a crew out there right now fixing the camera. But I apologize for any upsetment this caused you. Clearly someone is trying to intimidate you about writing anything that concerns Twin Oaks."

"Or about Nancy Harding's murder," Kara mumbled under her breath.

Kara's mind suddenly went into overdrive. Who had she told about putting Pa in Twin Oaks? Detective Cirelli. Jack. Joe Collins. Sue Butler. Nobody of consequence. Then there was the entire Twin Oaks staff. If it got out that the reporter writing about the Harding murder was Desmond Fitzgerald's daughter, any one of them with something to hide could have sent those cupcakes to scare the heck out of her. And it surely did.

Then there was Ricky Wexner. She had mentioned him in the piece as being Nancy's nephew and only living relative. It was inferred that he stood to inherit a great deal of her estate. She also mentioned that he had a drug problem, not new news as he had been in and out of rehab facilities all his life, but perhaps he was trying to reestablish his once wholesome image so he could work in G-rated pictures again.

"Miss Fitzgerald? Are you still there?'

"Yes, I'm here."

"I'm now worried," Mrs. Warren said softly, "that whoever sent those cupcakes will go a step further if your next story comes out."

Kara knew Mrs. Warren didn't want her to include the part about the arsenic, no matter how much she tried to convince her that it was a smart PR move. And who could blame her? But was she go to such lengths as to send the cupcakes to Pa herself?

"Let me talk with my editor," Kara stalled. "In the meantime, Mrs. Warren, I trust you will keep my father safe."

"Of course," Mrs. Warren answered tersely.

"Because if anything were to happen to him, you can just imagine what kind of story about Twin Oaks will next appear in the *Beacon*."

She hated herself for stooping to a veiled threat, but she wasn't about to roll over and back down as whoever sent those cupcakes wanted her to do.

Chapter Twenty-three

The Mullins pulled into the driveway. Kara waited until they were getting out of the faded gold sedan. Then she checked her purse, the side compartment where she had placed the "Jane Jones" letter.

When the Mullins were inside, Kara got out of the Civic and started up the gentle incline leading to the tidy house.

It felt a little like she was visiting family, people she knew well … even though she hardly knew the Mullins at all. There were simply "Jimmy's parents" to her growing up.

"Come in, Kara!" Mrs. Mullins opened the screen door. Kara caught a glimpse of Mr. Mullins. Like Pa, he was making a B-line for the TV. Gingerly. "I'll put the kettle on."

"I brought some crumb cake."

"Dear," Mrs. Mullins called into the living room. "did you hear that? Kara brought crumb cake. Your favorite!" But Mr. Mullins was lost in a world of grief. He barely acknowledged that there was a visitor. Kara's heart broke … for both of them.

"My Pa loves this crumb cake."

"How is your dear father?"

"He's at Twin Oaks. Dementia." Then she added, "But he seems to like it there."

"Well you be sure to tell him that the Mullins said hello. He is such a kind man."

"Yes. He is." Kara and Mrs. Mullins were now in the kitchen. *This is where Jimmy used to hang out*, she thought as she glanced around at the homey red and white checked pattern on the curtains and seat cushions. *This is where Jimmy ate breakfast. Maybe did his homework right where I'm sitting.*

Mrs. Mullins filled their tea cups as Kara sliced into the cake, making three cuts. "I'll take one into Mr. Mullins."

"Thank you, dear." Then Mrs. Mullins added, "Don't be upset if he appears to ignore you. He's working through troubling thoughts."

Kara nodded.

She found Mr. Mullins staring at a too loud TV. Grief, pure and contorted, was etched in his face. He looked tired. His soul tattered. Kara recognized this kind of grief. She saw it on Pa right after her mother died. And if her father had been left alone to wallow in it, he might have died himself shortly after he put his wife into the ground.

"Here you are, Mr. Mullins. It's nice and fresh," she left the slice on the small TV tray next to his chair. When she returned to the kitchen, she was glad to see that Mrs. Mullins was smiling. Her visit made a difference … at least for one of Jimmy's parents. It was a good moment.

"I hope you don't mind, Mrs. Mullins, but I'd like to show you something I just found among my mother's things. I thought you might be able to shed some light on it." She took the letter out of her purse. Mrs. Mullins stood up to get her reading glasses, then Kara watched as Mrs. Mullins perused the paper ... several times ... as if wanting to be sure of what she was reading.

"I never received a letter like this. Perhaps your mother meant to show it to me."

Kara realized that Mrs. Mullins had just verified what she had suspected.

"Did you know this Jane Jones?"

"I only met her once. At the hand over. That's what they called it. Your parents were there too." She paused and weakly smiled. "You didn't know that you and Jimmy were twins?"

"I only suspected it when I found this letter. I first became suspicious when I saw Jimmy's holy card … his birthdate. And then you mentioned at the wake how you and my mother would swap stories about us ... as babies." She paused. "Did my parents ever meet Jane Jones?"

"All four of us met her. Your parents, and Mr. Mullins and I. We knew right away that she was not the kind of person to have time to spend raising a child properly, much less two infants."

"You mean she was a teenager?"

"Not really. But young. And not interested in being a mother. She basically told us that outright ... though as you can see from the letter, she cared about both of you. Very much."

"Did you stay in touch with her?"

"Not really ... " It was an evasive response. Kara pressed.

"You mean you tried?"

"No. But there were a few times when I believed she was around. Keeping watch over our Jimmy. I mentioned it once to your mother and she said she had the same experience. You know, that she was keeping an eye on both of you from afar."

"You mean she was stalking us?"

"Oh, no, no, nothing like that at all! Please don't misunderstand. It's just that I would see a black car, like a limousine, lingering around the house, particularly when I would take Jimmy out for a walk in his stroller. Or once, when I brought him to the park to play on the swings ... I thought I saw that sane car in the parking lot. A chauffer was driving. I didn't see it a lot, mind you, but often enough. When Jimmy was little."

"And you thought it was Jane Jones in that car."

"I did. I suppose she may have wanted to be sure you and Jimmy were taken care of ... or maybe she was curious what you looked like. I don't know. Then, when Jimmy was about ten or eleven, it stopped. I suppose Jane needed to know that you were both loved." She reached across the table and touched Kara's hand. "Which you both were. Loved. Very, very much."

The remainder of the visit was bathed in a stretch of silence. It was clear to Kara that Mrs. Mullins was feeling the weight of grief. Kara stood to leave.

"Mrs. Mullins, you have been so kind to meet with me."

"No, no, dear. I should be thanking *you*. You are so thoughtful. And I hope I could help you a little bit. Sort things out? About the letter. "

"You helped me a lot."

"Please don't be a stranger, Kara. Mr. Mullins and I would be more than happy to see you any time. We're always around."

"I will stop by. And if I may ask you one more thing about Jimmy ... and me."

Mrs. Mullins' eyes widened. "Of course."

"Did Jimmy know I was his twin?"

"We told him when he reached the eighth grade. We knew the two of you would run into each other at Nelligan and we didn't want him to develop a crush on his own ... well, you understand." Then she smiled. "But we also told him that, because he was your big brother ... he was born a minute before you ... that he had to always look out for you"

"And he did look out for me," Kara said, hoping she wouldn't start crying. She had come here to comfort the Mullins ... not to have them comfort her.

"I'm so happy to know that."

It was time to leave. Her emotions were getting away from her. But Kara left with a new resolve ... a resolve to do everything in her power to find her brother's killer.

Chapter Twenty-four

After leaving the Mullins', Kara headed directly for Twin Oaks. She first wanted to see Pa, to give him a hug and make sure he knew how much she loved him. Life was far too short, and she had been recently reminded of that sad fact. The other reason was to see Mrs. Warren. They had ended their phone conversation abruptly and uncomfortably. Kara needed to be sure that there were no hard feelings. But she also had to stand firm that she would not white wash the Nancy Harding story. If there

But when she entered Mrs. Warren's posh office, she could tell immediately that the normally professional woman was distraught. "Did you see this?! One of my staffers saw it on the newsstand."

Kara could only see from a distance that it was a "Special Edition," put out in the early afternoon. It was a first, possibly a one-off, Kara thought. Jack was trying to drum up attention with a "special" afternoon printing. And he must have had it all planned before he went to Jimmy's funeral. Perhaps that is why Detective Cirelli was so angry at the gravesite.

Kara quickly perused the story. It was another sensational, speculative piece by Jack suggesting that Nancy Harding's killer had to be someone working within the confines of Twin Oaks. That they would be the only individual with access to the cupcakes.

"This is not what I wanted," Kara said defensively. "You read my piece. My editor is going rogue, trying to drum up circulation by printing opinion. I am so sorry."

"He has to be stopped, Kara. I have a good mind to have our attorney sue him."

"I understand. But he does state up front in the piece that this is an editorial. I don't know if you have grounds for a lawsuit."

"I don't care what it is. My staff has been with me for years … some longer than a decade. For the first time this morning a few of them threatened to quit."

"But they know you and the police don't suspect any of them," Kara said, leaving off the word "yet" at the end of her statement. "I'll talk to him. But for what it's worth, the police aren't too thrilled with him either." Kara thumbed through the rest of the light "flyer." There was another editorial about Father Dunleavy's theory, this time listing the names of all the priests who had ever been considered by the Archdiocese to be elevated to bishop, which was most likely what got Detective Cirelli miffed, and basically accused them of conspiring to get Father Mullins out of the way.

Kara sighed with frustration. Jack was out of control.

"When you called me about the cupcakes delivered to my father … did you tell the police about them?"

"Yes. Well, I intended to, then Daniel came into my office and showed me this awful story. Then the switchboard blew up and I got deluged with calls from anxious family members.." She paused. "It's only quiet now because I redirected the calls to my secretary. Poor thing."

"But you told me on the phone that the police were checking the box for fingerprints."

"I presumed that's what they would do." She blushed. Kara knew she'd caught her in a lie. "But I shall call them immediately. My secretary has the cupcakes and the box they came in.

Same kind of box from Vitale's. Now that I think about it, that box probably now has my fingerprints as well as hers."

"The police will sort that out. And what you told me about there being no arsenic. How did you know that if the police hadn't yet tested them?'

"I'm sorry. I didn't want to alarm you."

"Mrs. Warren," Kara held in her fury. "Please call the police now or I will call them myself." Mrs. Warren nodded anxiously. Kara was still whirling with anger. She drew in a breath then walked toward the dining room. Hopefully, Pa would be enjoying his afternoon snack with his friends. And when she found him, he was … happily holding court at the same table with the same affable guys. Kara figured Pa's stale jokes were going over so well for the third or fourth time because most of the men at his table were just as forgetful as he was.

Kara found Daniel seated nearby. She approached. At first, he barely made eye contact.

"Daniel, I want you to know that the story you saw in the *Beacon,* well, I knew nothing about it."

He looked at her. "I find that hard to believe."

"It's true. My editor is desperate, trying to raise circulation numbers. I'm afraid he went overboard. If it makes you feel any better, I think the world of you and the staff here … and I plan to write my own editorial about that, and how well you and everyone at Twin Oaks is caring for my Pa."

Daniel looked up and, for the first time, his eyes met hers. "You'll do that?"

"I think I need to. Yes." She could only pray that Jack would not interfere. And while Kara wasn't sure she had convinced Daniel that she would try to make things right, she couldn't prove it until he saw it in print. Now it was time for her to talk with Detective Cirelli. She placed the call from her car.

"Mrs. Warren just called me," Cirelli began. "I've sent one of our guys over to Twin Oaks to pick up the cupcakes sent to your father and do a fingerprint analysis on the box. How is your father doing?"

"I just saw him. He's in his own world. Which is a good thing, I guess."

"Yes. It is. And for what it's worth, Kara, I chewed Jack out." Then he added, "He's not himself lately."

Kara wasn't sure what Jack's "self" was really like, but she knew for certain that Detective Cirelli was worried about him and his desperate antics. Jack was acting out of fear … fear of losing his job and the work that had sustained him since he was a teenager. If he had a wife or family or a few close friends, Kara knew he wouldn't be prone to resort to such despondent measures. But he was ruining his reputation and the reputation of the *Beacon* as the last bastion of real journalism in north Jersey.

"He's frightened of losing his job, Detective. Acting desperate." Kara said, but she knew that, despite the fact that Cirelli still trusted her with inside information, his days of giving "exclusives" to the *Beacon* were over … thanks to Jack. Then she added, "If you find arsenic in the cupcakes sent to my Pa …" she hesitated.

"Are you asking if I think your father is safe at Twin Oaks? Because if that's what you're asking, Kara, then my answer is I don't know. I really don't know" Then he added, "But

I've known Mrs. Warren for years. She goes to our church. She won't let another person in her care fall prey to foul play."

"And Ricky Wexner. Do you think he had a hand in any of this?"

"Between us, Kara, and I know I can trust *you* … " he paused … "I'm not convinced that Wexner had anything to do with his aunt's murder. My guys called me from Boca last night after speaking with Wexner for hours. He's not the sharpest tack in the box. If you know what I mean."

"You don't think he'd be capable of murder?"

"I don't think he killed his aunt. It doesn't make sense She was good to him. And though he has a drug problem, my guys got the impression that he relied on her. He had nobody else. She was his only family. She was financing him … and she was very generous."

"Well somebody out there wants to keep your attention on Ricky."

"I know, Kara. I know."

Chapter Twenty-five

Detective Cirelli hung up the phone and took a sip of coffee. It wasn't the good stuff that Bridget made at home. He'd forgotten to bring the thermos she filled for him each morning. No, this was the burnt junk at the bottom of the pot that had been sitting there for … well, long enough to taste awful but not long enough to start growing fuzz. He put the mug down and decided it was a good day to cut down on coffee. Besides, his nerves didn't need any help in feeling frayed.

After a decades long career in law enforcement filled with burglaries and domestic abuse cases, here was not one but two murders …a former Hollywood movie star and a beloved priest, and both cases were going nowhere. Cirelli wasn't even counting, yet, the sudden, suspicious heart attack of old Father Dunleavy. The poor old priest went to his grave believing firmly that a fellow man of the cloth, a jealous cleric, murdered Father Mullins because the young man was on the fast track to becoming a bishop, beating out those who had supposedly "put in their time." Was the old priest on to something, he wondered.

And then there was Jack Logan. Cirelli was concerned. He'd known Jack all his life and didn't like what he was becoming. Cirelli and Jack's adoptive father, John Logan, started out on the force at the same time. They were even partners for a while. And Cirelli was on duty the day they found a little boy, abandoned, filthy, starving and tearful … a memory Cirelli would never forget. The Logans adopted the child and Logan treated him as well, if not better, than his six older kids. He even brought the boy into the precinct every now and then. Little Jack was a sweet but shy kid. For a while, he wanted to become a cop like his old man. Then, some time in high school, he got the journalism bug and that was the end of any interest in a career in law enforcement. Now, with the desperate way Jack was acting, Cirelli was grateful that he never did become an officer of the law. Jack was using the *Beacon* to play fast and loose with the facts. He even broke the bond that he and the detective had when it came to sharing information. No longer could Jack be trusted with the inside track on anything. It was a disappointment to Cirelli who always held a soft spot in his heart for Jack.

Cirelli inadvertently picked up the coffee mug and almost took another sip of the foul brew it contained. Bridget's coffee had spoiled him. But soon, with retirement just around the corner, he'd be enjoying her coffee every morning. At home. In the kitchen he and she planned to renovate. The kitchen renovation which, like retirement, was long overdue.

Lost in his daydream, Cirelli realized that he was staring at a report that the precinct secretary had left on his desk. It contained the notes that his guys down in Boca had called in. They were convinced, after hours of interrogation, that Ricky Wexner could no longer be considered a person of interest in his aunt's death. Wexner was under constant surveillance at the rehab center he entered just before Nancy Harding ate those poisoned cupcakes. Even if he wanted to direct someone to deliver the arsenic laced sweets from afar, he couldn't. The center had a strict policy and did not allow cell phones. All of the rooms and common spaces were monitored by closed circuit TV and each patient was assigned a personal assistant who kept watch over them twenty-four seven. No way could Wexner pull it off, even if he wanted to. Cirelli had to agree with his guys. He took Wexner's name off of his suspect list … which left a question mark. Was it someone on staff? He had to find someone with a motive. He had to find out who could possibly benefit from Nancy Harding dying.

Cirelli looked over his notes again. His officers had talked to the baker at Vitale's who said the cupcakes that killed Nancy were ordered by phone with a request to leave them outside the bake shop at 10pm, after closing. The guys were working on getting the records of incoming calls on the baker's landline. And, unfortunately, the bakery, an old establishment run by the same family for a hundred years, did not have CCTV outside. Whoever ordered the cupcakes knew the workings of the bakery when they requested that they be left outside the store at ten o'clock, after closing. Vitale's always left their day old bread outside their shop after closing for the local homeless shelter and soup kitchen to pick up. Could it be someone who worked for the shelter or soup kitchen?

All Cirelli knew for certain was that someone picked up those cupcakes, inserted the arsenic, then took them to Twin Oaks to be left, in the dead of night, on the front stoop with Nancy's name on them. Still, the most important question was yet to be answered … who would do such a thing … and why? Who stood to gain something from Nancy Harding's death? From all his decades of experience, Cirelli knew that the best way to find the answer to that question was to follow the money. He had to get a copy of Nancy's will. So far, he was not having any luck in tracking it down. Mrs. Warren said she would do a clean sweep of Nancy's room. The police had already cleared it as a crime scene and found nothing, but perhaps they missed it.

Cirelli put aside the Harding file and turned his attention to the Father Mullins case. He wanted to reread the interviews he and his team conducted with the three couples who attended the marriage retreat at the Hague mansion. He had read them umpteenth times already, but was convinced there was something he was missing.

The three couples were an odd bunch, to be sure. Entitled, born into upper middle class privilege, and out of touch with the common touch. But was a killer among them?

They had gone on the retreat to fix their marriages. But how do you "fix" a marriage? He couldn't relate as he subscribed to the notion that if it wasn't right from the get-go, it was never going to be right.

He and his Bridget had been married for nearly forty years and never once needed any kind of retreat or counselling to navigate the ups and downs of their shared life. They both believed that marriage was a commitment to God that they would do their best for each other. And for the past forty years, that philosophy worked, supplemented with heavy doses of love, respect and trust. He adored her and she treated him like her best friend. And, if something ever bothered either of them, they could always sit down and hash it out, sometimes loudly, but still respectfully ... and in a few hours, or the next morning, they'd be back to being the best of friends. But these couples ... it seemed to Cirelli that they were looking for some ideal of perfection they, or at least the women, saw in one of those Hallmark Christmas movies his daughters used to watch.

The phone rang. His private line. He only gave out this number to a few people, people whose cases he was working on. It was Mrs. Warren.

"Detective, I just remembered something. During one of his visits, Daniel and I overheard Nancy and her nephew arguing loudly about her will."

"Arguing?" Cirelli's ears perked up.

"Well, discussing it … loudly. Something about her threatening Ricky that if didn't go into rehab, she was going to cut him out of her will. That's all."

"Hmmm …" Cirelli made a mental note. "But you haven't found a will among Miss Harding's things."

"No. But have you spoken with Nancy's accountant?"

"I don't follow."

"Her accountant was also her executor. Dennis Gregson."

Cirelli knew that name. Gregson was one of the people on the marriage retreat. "Gregson is Harding's executor?" Gregson and his wife were at Father Mullins wake but, oddly, not at his funeral.. And now it seemed strange to Cirelli that, throughout all of the times he and the others were interrogated about Father Mullins' murder, Gregson never once revealed that he worked for Nancy Harding, or that he had a copy of her will.

The will held clues. Gregson had to know that. Who else stood to benefit from Nancy's demise? Cirelli could only discern one thing, that Gregson's silence spoke volumes about his possible guilt. Why else would he hide his association with Nancy? His connection to her estate? Unless he stood to gain from it. Now Gregson was on the top of Cirelli's hit list. He was the guy who was involved with both of the victims.

"I just thought that bit of information might be helpful."

"Very helpful. Thank you." He hung up, his mind racing. Why didn't Gregson tell the police that he was the executor of Nancy Harding's will if he had nothing to hide? Cirelli thought about the odd couple he saw at the wake. The glamorous wife and the milquetoast husband.

"Oh, I nearly forgot to ask. I received a call just a few moments ago," Mrs. Wexner added. "From Ricky Wexner. He wants to bury his aunt and wondered if I knew when the police would be releasing Nancy's body. He'd like to have her cremated."

Cirelli wondered why Wexner wouldn't simply call the police directly. He had spoken to several of the officers at length and surely had their direct cell numbers.

"We're not releasing the body yet, but I'll have one of my guys call him about it," Cirelli replied tersely, then hung up. His attention returned to the Mullins' file where he found the interview that was conducted with Dennis Gregson. Not once did he mention his relationship with Nancy Harding. What was this guy hiding, Cirelli wondered. Whatever it was, he was determined to find out.

Chapter Twenty-six

When Kara got home, her first order of business was to make herself a strong cup of tea. She was furious and disappointed with Jack. But despite the temptation to "straighten him out" and remind him about his own commitment, once upon a time, to solid journalism, she knew she had to pick her battles carefully. She needed to make money, and right now writing assignments for the *Beacon* were her only means to sustain herself. She literally couldn't afford to get on Jack's bad side. Then, just as she was about to warm up the kettle for a second cup, she heard what sounded like a large truck outside. Suddenly she remembered. She had called several charities to donate her parents' bulky furniture and here was one of them, coming for the living and dining rooms as well as all the beds. And while it pained her to part with the memories … Pa's favorite chair, her mother's hope chest, it was necessary. Days were ticking by before closing on the house and she needed the place to be immaculately sparse.

A quick peek through the front window allowed her a chuckle. The two moving guys could be stand-ins for Laurel and Hardy. Fat and skinny. How on earth would they be able to carry all this stuff, she wondered. But they got to work. First on the living room, then the dining room, then upstairs.

"They don't make 'em like this anymore," the heavy one remarked as he carried Kara's Salem maple bed through the front door. Kara sipped her fourth cup of tea and wondered how she was going to get a good night's sleep tonight without even as much as a blow-up mattress. When the guys finished, only three throw pillows and a couple of shawls her mother crocheted remained. In the bright autumn daylight, the rooms looked … well … sad. Their personality went out the door with the furniture. And that made Kara feel sad too.

"Oh, well, Little Grey. It's just us now," Kara said, feeling tears beginning to well in her eyes. Somehow seeing Pa's chair leave the house was just as bad as how she felt the other day when she took him to Twin Oaks.

She glanced over the receipt the men handed her. They said something about her being able to deduct the items on her taxes. She had signed it quickly, but really felt no need to look. But there, on top, were the words "Catholic Charities."

Catholic Charities. Catholic Charities. Why were those words rumbling around her head? Then she remembered. Wasn't that the same organization that arranged adoptions? She remembered her mother saying that many times, but when she asked her mother if Catholic Charities arranged *her* adoption, Ann Fitzgerald clammed up. Now Kara believed that she and Jimmy's adoptions must have been arranged through Catholic Charities.

She could check it out with Mrs. Mullins, but she didn't want to impose on the women in her time of grief. Instead, Kara gave it a try and placed a call to the charity.

"But our records are private and sealed, " a no-nonsense administrator said as if she'd said those same words dozens and dozens of times before to dozens and dozens of adopted children who wanted to grasp a branch of their family tree.

"You see, I was a twin but we were adopted separately. He recently died ……. he was actually murdered."

"Oh, dear," the woman gasped.

"I thought … well, if our birth mother heard the news … it was in the media … well, I have reason to believe she would recognize my brother's name. I thought it might comfort her to learn that her other child was still alive … and fine."

"I'm sorry but …" then she hesitated. "Let me check something." The phone went quiet but Kara could hear the sound of typing on a keyboard in the background. Then: "Miss, you said your birth mother's name was Jane Jones?"

"Yes!" Kara answered quickly, hopefully. "Because I just typed the name Jane Jones into our database and nothing came up."

"But … and you typed in our birthdate? We were born on April 23rd, 1990."

"I'm sorry. I still don't see anything."

"Can you check again?"

The woman rambled on about privacy and that there were some birth mothers, especially very young ones, who didn't want their children to find them and would give aliases.

"So her name might not be Jane Jones?"

"I'm just saying that some birth mothers, teenagers in particular, have been known to do that. Change their name. They want to get on with their lives, marry someone, have more children, and forget their past."

Her words stung Kara's heart. If this "Jane Jones" wanted to move on, to forget about her and Jimmy, then why would she be keeping an eye on them from a distance, as Mrs. Mullins said. It didn't make sense. "I'm very sorry, Miss, but I cannot help you any further."

But Kara wasn't about to give up so easily. Her years covering crime kicked in. She could tell by the abrupt change in the woman's tone of voice that she came upon something in the files. Something she was hiding.

"Please tell me what you just found." Kara pleaded. "I just learned that the boy I knew throughout my school years was actually my brother, my twin, and now he's been brutally murdered. Nothing you found in your files can shock me." There was a long pause. Silence. Kara interpreted it as a sign of hope. Then … "I … I just found the name of a woman in our files who gave up two children, twins, a boy and a girl, in late April of 1990."

"Can you tell me her real name?"

"I don't even know if she is the right person. She noted here that she did not want to be contacted."

"If the birth was twins, a boy and a girl, on April 23rd, then that has to be my birth mother. And chances are she is grieving, that she knows one of her babies was killed. I can comfort her."

"But it may not be your mother. I see here that she gave up another child for adoption at the same time."

"*Another* child?" Kara was suddenly taken off her game. She *couldn't* be one of triplets. Mrs. Mullins would have told her. But what if Mrs. Mullins didn't know about another child? If she and Jimmy were newborns, maybe this child was older?

"Can you tell me anything about the other child? I mean, I could have a brother or sister out there … it would be nice having just lost one sibling … please give me a break."

"I'm sorry. I've told you too much already. This woman might not even be your mother."

But Kara knew in her heart that it was. She put the phone down. She was numb. Somewhere out there was a sibling. And a birth mother who, perhaps, needed her forgiveness, and maybe her love. And she had no way of finding them.

A deep sense of sadness suddenly swept over her. Then again, should she be angry? What kind of woman could give away three children? Then, in the next moment, she answered her own question … a desperate woman … or a very selfish one.

She put the phone down, then noticed that she had a message from Sue Butler. A text. "You moving into the cottage? Need to know. Hope so!"

Kara owed Sue an answer … which was, of course, "yes!" She put aside her curiosity and frustration about her birth mother. Temporarily. It was time to get things in gear. Sue was anxious to have someone living in her cottage before her husband moved in. Kara knew that if she didn't act quickly, Sue would find another tenant.

She glanced around the empty house. All that was left was to move the boxes of nick-nacks and family hcirlooms into a storage facility, then pack up herself and Little Grey.

She got to work, carrying some of the brown packing boxes out to her car. The only thing she forgot to repack was her old Nelligan yearbook. She had taken it out of the closet when she heard Jimmy died. Now, glancing through the pages, especially the pictures of Jimmy, she felt the pain of what she never had. A brother. And there he was all the time. Larger than life. Shooting hoops, dancing at the prom with Cindy, on the debate team, washing cars to raise money for local causes. Her brother, she proudly smiled, tears falling down her cheeks.

And there *she* was, always in the background. Shy and reclusive, a shadow of the person she was to become. Even her senior portrait was a testament to her fear of flying through life. A gentle face with a soft smile camouflaged by the crazed confusion that sprouted in the head of old Sister Angelina who Kara, trying to be kind, asked to sign her yearbook. But when the old nun asked to see her portrait, which Kara turned to proudly, Sister picked up her Shaeffer fountain pen and proceeded to scroll "May you follow the Good Lord always" all over Kara's face. It still miffed her to think of it. Did any of the other students have Sister Angelina's penmanship scrolled all over their visage? She thought not. They were too cool to even ask the old nun to sign. *That's what you get for being too nice*, she scolded herself.

To her friends, upon seeing the desecration, it was a joke. But to Kara, it was just another reminder that she could never be one of the cool kids. Now it was a painful reminder of the vast divide between the person she was back at Nelligan and the person she had become. If only she knew then what she knew now. But wasn't that always the way? She slammed the yearbook shut. But as Kara slid it into a space in one of the packing boxes, she had no idea that she had just packed away a significant clue in solving not one but two murders.

Chapter Twenty-seven

"What do you mean he's out of town?" Detective Cirelli snapped at one of his officers. It wasn't like him to lose his cool, but the officer had allowed two "persons of interest" in both the Harding and the Mullins murders to slip out of town without alerting the police.

Dennis Gregson and his wife had been at the wake. Visually, he found the couple amusing. The contrast between the "hen" and the "hen pecked" was clear. She was wrapped in diamonds and designer duds while he trailed along, a sliver of a man, with the sex appeal of a salamander.

"Find them … find them both. Tell them I need a copy of the Harding will. Pronto! Or I'll send my team to his business and his home with a search warrant."

He took another sip of cold coffee, the bad stuff, and almost didn't notice. He was that angry.

Thanks to Jack Logan and his desperate attempt to boost the *Beacon*'s circulation numbers, the Archdiocese had gone dark in the Mullins case. Not that they were cooperating fully before, but now that the news was out and the innuendo, that Father Mullins was murdered by a jealous priest, was in the headlines, the Archdiocese was closing ranks.

"Detective? We just tracked down Gregson. He's at his summer home in Spring Lake. He's drivin' back now and should be here in an hour."

"Good. Make sure you bring him to see me as soon as he arrives." Detective Cirelli paused. "Doesn't he realize he's my lead suspect in two murder cases?" It was a rhetorical question.

The rookie cop didn't realize that. "I don't think he knows that, Detective."

"Well he will when I finish questioning him."

Chapter Twenty-eight

Kara had just packed away her yearbook when the doorbell rang. It was the last person she expected to see … Jack. He was carrying a bouquet of lovely flowers and wearing a remorseful expression … both out of character for the normally hard crusted editor. "I'm still on Cirelli's shit list," he huffed as he helped himself inside.

"Are those for anyone in particular?" Kara teased.

"Oh, yeah, they're for you." He handed them over like he was tossing her a hot potato. She smiled. This was a rare, softer, apologetic side of Jack. At least she *hoped* the flowers were for that reason. She prayed he suddenly hadn't become romantically interested in her … which would be an awful, clumsy situation.

"They're beautiful But what are they for?"

"They're an apology. Because you were right ..."

"Come again?" she teased with a smile as she led him to the kitchen where she put the flowers in water.

"I mean about keeping quiet about the Mullins murder. Cirelli really chewed me out."

"Jack, I'm not gonna rub salt in the wound, but you know better than I that if the police tell us to keep quiet about a case they have good reason. Maybe the Archdiocese has a suspect and didn't want a news report to put the individual on guard." She paused. "And now you've opened a Pandora's box about how old Father Dunleavy died." She felt herself losing her composure. "Jack, you know better. If the *Beacon* becomes another tabloid, why would our loyal readers want to buy us anymore?"

"Cirelli will come around. He promised my father that he'd always keep an eye on me."

"Well out of respect for your father and the detective, stop writing stories full of hearsay and innuendo. Stick to the facts. That's what you always taught me." She paused. "Try calling Detective Cirelli again. Offer a sincere apology. But don't send him flowers," she joked. He didn't even crack a smile. Jack, she realized, had no sense of humor.

"Would you? Talk to him?" Jack said sheepishly. Kara suddenly knew the real reason for the flowers. Not so much to say sorry for trying to pressure her into abandoning her journalistic integrity in the Nancy Harding stories, but to get her to bring Detective Cirelli around so he wouldn't start giving exclusives to their competitor, the *Jersey Herald*.

"If I talk to the detective and promise that we won't jump the gun on any future stories, do I have your word that you won't? Because if you put me under the bus …"

"I won't. And thanks." He paused. "How's your Pa doing?" It was a strange segue for Jack to take. He hardly knew Pa.

"He's fine."

"Good."

"And one more thing Jack."

"Yeah?"

"When can I expect to be paid? I'm really strapped for cash right now."

"Who isn't?"

"But you have a job."

"For the time being." He paused. "But yeah … you'll get paid the standard fee for a stringer … should keep the wolf from the door for a little while. I'll get a check cut later today."

"Thanks." She paused, collecting her words. "And one more thing."

"Yeah?"

"When we get the okay from the police, I was thinking of writing a tribute piece of Jimmy."

Jack looked at her strangely. "Why?"

"Because he was a good guy. A really fine priest. And …" she dropped the bombshell … "I just learned he was my twin brother."

Jack visibly did a double take. "What?"

"I know. I just learned that Jimmy and I were twins. All these years I had a brother and never knew it. I mean, what are the chances?" Jack simply stared at her … stunned. His normally pale skin grew even paler, accentuating his dark eyes and brows. In many ways, Jack Logan was a very handsome man, Kara thought in that moment. If he didn't have such a dour personality. It camouflaged his outstanding features. "You look like you're in shock!" Kara giggled. "Isn't that wild?'

"Yeah. Wow ... that is ... yeah … I mean, how did you find out?"

"Never mind that, but it's been verified by a very reliable source. Anyway, when the dust settles and the police find Jimmy's killer, well, I would like to honor my brother with a piece about him."

"You make him sound like he was a saint."

"Well, yes. To me, he was. Or more like my Guardian Angel. Always showing up to rescue me. To help me when I needed him. It was uncanny. Like the bond between twins was always there … only I never knew it."

"Did he know? That you were his twin?"

"He knew. The Mullins told him. I wish my folks had told me."

He hesitated. "Are you sure it would be safe … I mean to write such a thing?" It wasn't like Jack to turn down a good story. And this promised to be a really good one.

"What do you mean?"

"I mean, don't get me wrong, but the cops might never find Mullins' killer. You might be putting yourself in danger if you tell the world you're related to him."

"I never thought of that," she mused. Jack had a good point. He was protecting her, as it wasn't like Jack Logan to turn down a good story.

"Think about it, Fitz. Whoever killed Mullins could have it out for anyone associated with him."

He was right, of course. As long as Jimmy's murderer was out there, she could be his next victim. Guilt by association, she thought. It was a terrifying thought.

Chapter Twenty-nine

Jack had no sooner left when the phone buzzed. The caller I.D. read J. Collins.

"Hi!"

"Hey, Kara. I don't know about you but I didn't eat all day. You feel like grabbing a burger at the Dubliner? You haven't lived till you've tried the Dublin burger with spicy fries."

"Sounds like an offer I can't refuse. Give me twenty minutes, deal?"

"Deal. Meet you on your patio in twenty."

Kara wasted no time getting ready. If there was one person who could lift her out of the melancholy she was feeling it was Joe. He seemed like a genuinely happy person. And he was easy on the eyes. Not a bad combination.

After a quick rinse off in the shower, Kara put on a new lavender cashmere sweater and a pair of jeans, then slipped into flats. A few Velcro rollers in her hair lifted it enough to style. Then she applied a fresh coat of makeup. Or "shellac" as Pa called it. When she took a glance at the finished product in the full length mirror, she smiled ... until she realized that she nearly went out the door with two of the Velcro rollers clinging to the neckline of her sweater.

If this was a date, she thought, then so be it. But there was something so comfortable about being around Joe that she didn't care if this was just two new friends enjoying each other's company or something more serious. At the moment, it just felt right.

When Kara opened the drapes to the patio, she found Joe waiting. He too had made an effort. He looked handsome. Tan slacks. Jacket. Open collared shirt.

"Ready?" he smiled as she opened the sliding glass door.

Little Grey suddenly appeared at her ankle, then tip-toed across the patio and brushed against Joe's pant leg. "Well hello there," he greeted the tiny kitten then bent down to caress her fur. "She remembers me."

"Of course she does," Kara smiled. "But she can't come to the Dubliner with us."

"You hear that?" he picked up the kitten in one hand and promptly brought her to the patio door. "No burgers and fries for you." Kara locked the door then followed Joe through both backyards to his truck, parked in his drive. It was a shiny dark blue pick-up. Most likely the one he used for his work but now spic and span.

When they arrived at the Dubliner, the crowd was engrossed in a Giants game on the TV monitors that were banked behind the bar and near the ceiling of the dining room. Joe greeted the bartender, "Eddy," then nodded to a booth at the back. Kara was impressed that Joe chose to sit on the side that didn't face the wide screen TVs, a sign that he wanted to focus solely on *her*.

"How's the move going? I noticed you got rid of your furniture."

"Guess I'll be sleeping on the carpet tonight," came out of her mouth and she suddenly realized that it could be misinterpreted, that she was hinting to stay with him. She wasn't that kind of girl. But Joe seemed to know it already..

"So you plan to move soon?"

"I still need to follow up with my friend. I can stay with her until I get a steady job. Then I'll get my own place."

"That sounds smart. But is it strange? I mean, being alone in the house without your father around? I'm sure it's an adjustment. Being without family." It was an innocent enough remark, but it launched Kara into thoughts of one particular person in her family. She didn't need more encouragement to open up about Jimmy.

She shared everything, about Jimmy's murder, finding the holy card with the date of his birth, Mrs. Mullins confirming that they were twins, and how it all tied back to the Jane Jones letter.

"I even have another sibling somewhere out there. Another child that Jane Jones gave up."

Joe was temporarily speechless, then he reached across the booth and gently placed a hand over hers.. "I don't know what to say, Kara. It's surreal." Then: "I hope you find your birth mother. And your other sibling. I really do."

"Thank you."

"And your Pa. You're sure he's okay at Twin Oaks?"

Kara knew Joe meant well, that he was genuinely concerned for Pa's safety. But Kara didn't have much of a choice. Especially now with the date for the house closing looming large. "I thought about that. But I figured they run a business. And they can't afford for him or any of their guests NOT to be okay. Safe. I'm sure they're beefing up security."

"But if you had a choice, you'd keep your home and bring your Pa back to live there."

Kara exhaled. "Absolutely." Then: "But I can't. Not without home care. Twenty-four seven. And I can't afford that. That's the whole point of selling the house. To be able to afford his care."

"I understand." And he did. Which made Kara feel better just being able to share her situation with someone she felt she could trust. Someone who really listened. And someone, she thought, who cared.

She looked down at her plate. Her burger was three-fourths done and she didn't remember taking a single bite. "Enough about me."

"You live a much more interesting life," Joe chuckled. "And I think you're very strong, Kara, and you will come through all of this to a better place. I even think you'll find your sibling."

"You do?"

"I do. I don't know why I do but I think you will. In fact, I think everything you want you will eventually get."

She didn't press him about why he said what he did. Maybe he was just being kind, she thought, trying to put a positive spin on things.

As they walked to the parking lot, Joe gently touched her arm. "Will you give me your new address? At your friend's place?"

"Yes. Sure." She waited while he took out his phone. She gave him Sue's address and he put it into his phone.

"I like it out there. Country Estates. All that fresh air. Acres of nothing but farmland, horses." He then looked up from his phone and into her eyes. "We'll stay in touch, right?"

"Of course." She smiled.

"And don't worry about anything, Kara. I'm a big believer that things have a way of working out exactly as they were meant to be."

And perhaps Joe was right, she thought. At least his words made her feel better, as if things might actually be turning out exactly as they were meant to. He bent down to kiss her cheek. It had been a lovely evening … just what she needed. And as they made small talk on the ride home, then said goodnight with a wave, Kara had a feeling that she just met someone who was going to play a very important role in her life. Maybe the *most* important role.

Chapter Thirty

Kara had no sooner put her purse and cell on the kitchen counter when a call came in. She didn't have to look at the caller I.D. Only Jack Logan would be calling at this hour.

"Jack, don't you ever sleep?"

"I could ask you the same thing." There was an awkward pause. "Hey, you been talkin' with Cirelli?"

Kara's guard suddenly went up. "What are you asking?"

"He tell you anything? About that nephew of Nancy Harding's?"

"Just that he's no longer a person of interest." Then: "Any chance you can speed up my check? I'm literally broke."

"I'm workin' on it." He paused. "You get me some inside info from Cirelli and maybe I can get you on staff again."

Truth be told, Kara was starting to change how she felt about returning to the *Beacon*. But she didn't tell Jack. In fact, it was because of Jack that she felt this way. He was changing everything about the paper because of insecurities about his own position. The standards were going down the drain. And that isn't why Kara became a journalist. But where she would go … well, she knew there were really no other options. The tabloids were cut from the same cloth. Drek. Journalism was going down the toilet, and the pressure to sell papers and lie if necessary was too much for her sensibilities. "I still think the nephew is involved."

"Not Dennis Gregson?" Kara countered. "I mean, there's no proof, but I'd think Detective Cirelli is keeping a sharp eye on that guy. I mean, he's clearly under pressure to keep

Cindy in designer clothes and expensive cars. He's the only person who knew both Nancy and Jimmy. He could have been jealous. Maybe Cindy still harbors a crush on Jimmy. I mean, what prompted Dennis and Cindy to attend that marriage retreat if their marriage wasn't in trouble? Maybe Cindy threatened to leave him. I'm just spit balling, Jack, but if I were Cirelli I'd be looking into what Gregson gets paid for being executor of Nancy's will."

"That rookie at the precinct. You know, the one who blabs. I think she has a crush on me." He was serious and Kara refrained from laughing. Though Jack on the surface was a good-looking guy, even handsome to some, once any woman was around him for a few minutes, his appearance transformed from Hot Hunk into Hopeless Hulk.

"Oh, really?"

"Anyhow, she told me that Cirelli is tryin' to get a copy of Harding's will. He's gonna follow the money. See how much Gregson stands to inherit."

"So as both Nancy's executor and her accountant, the police believe that Gregson stands to inherit a big chunk of her money just for his services. Even though he's not one of her heirs."

"Yeah. That's what the rookie told me. That's why Cirelli wants that will. To find out how much money we're talkin' about."

"And you think that if you hand over the will to the police before they pry it from Gregson, that you'll be back in Cirelli's good graces."

"Yeah. Kind of like that." He paused. "Fitz, you've gotta get your hands on that will. You find it pronto and then I'll have a reason to insist my publisher give you your old job back."

"I thought you said there were money issues with hiring full timers."

"There are. But if we can print parts of Harding's will on the front page, the *Beacon* will fly off the newsstands. People like that kind of crap. A peek into the mindset of a movie star with money. See how much money the rich and famous leave behind."

"Jack, I can't see people shelling out two bucks just to read that. Besides, we don't know for sure if Nancy Harding was still rich. If she had anything left to her name."

"Doesn't matter. People like to read that crap. They'll shell out two bucks. Easy. Now, can you get your hands on the will?"

"And how am I supposed to do that?"

"It's a safe bet that whoever cleaned out Harding's room after she kicked the bucket found a copy of the will. I'll bet a six pack that that director ..."

"Mrs. Warren?"

"Yeah. Her. I'll bet she has a copy."

"But if she does, why wouldn't she turn it over to the police?"

"Because I'll bet there's somethin' in there that she doesn't want the police to know. Just like why Gregson is playing hard to get. Someone stands to gain a lot of money ... not just Wexner."

"Maybe you're right. But that doesn't make that person a murderer."

"Or maybe it does."

Kara hung up, not sure how or if she would try to find a copy of Nancy Harding's will. Her first thought was that if the police couldn't get a copy from Gregson, why would she have

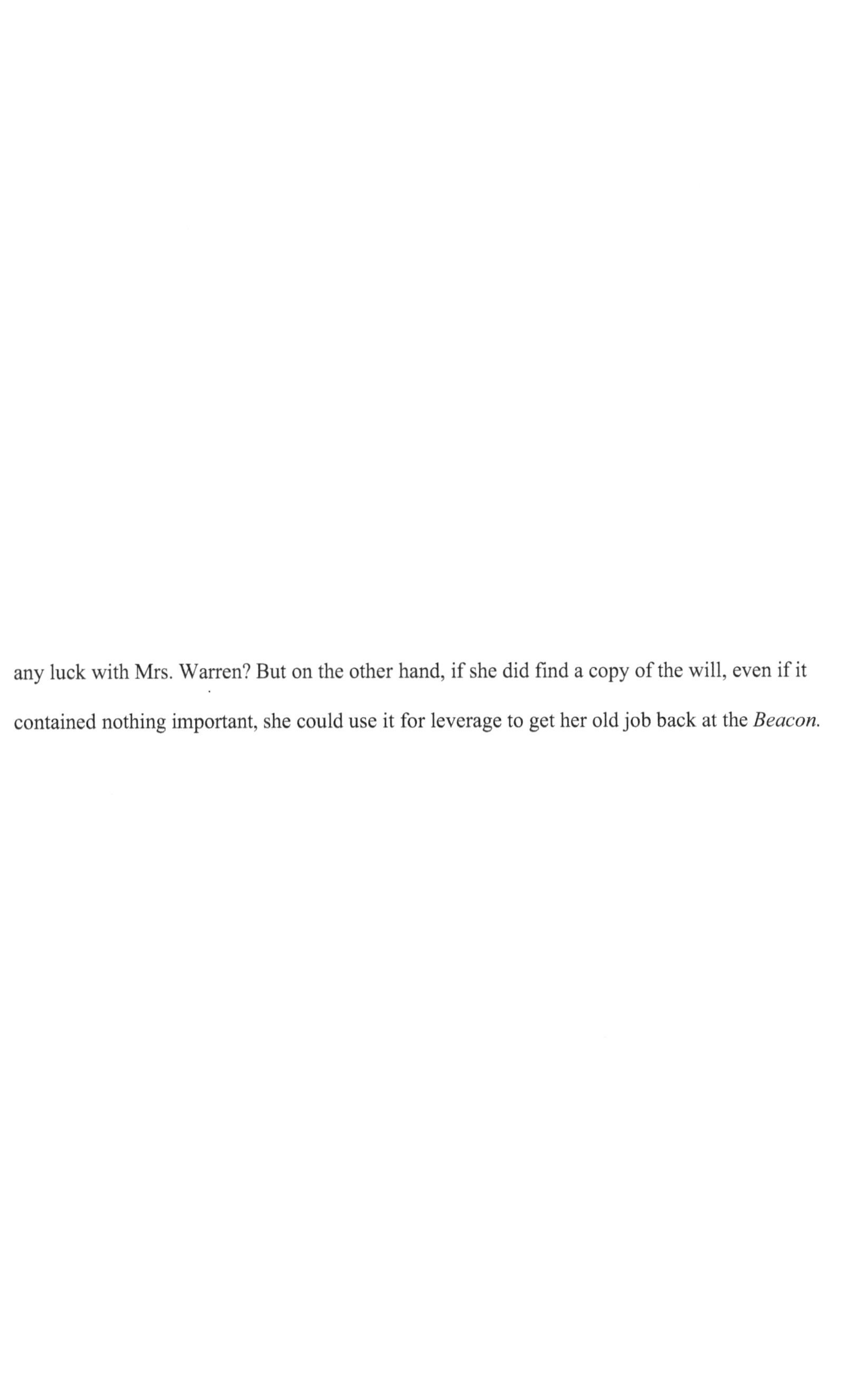

any luck with Mrs. Warren? But on the other hand, if she did find a copy of the will, even if it

contained nothing important, she could use it for leverage to get her old job back at the *Beacon*.

Chapter Thirty-one

Darkness settled over the house. The only illumination was a light over the stove in the kitchen and a family of nightlights, one plugged into each downstairs socket. Kara was bone tired. Her pleasant mood, buoyed by a lovely dinner with a new, good friend had been ruined by Jack's phone call. Her mind raced with thoughts about Dennis Gregson and why he would be slow in producing Nancy Harding's will for the police. What was there to hide? Unless, of course, he was due a larger chunk of the proceeds beyond his customary fee. That might raise police suspicions.

Besides his role as Nancy's executor and accountant, Kara wondered if milquetoast Dennis was the jealous type. But jealous enough to suspect his wife still harbored a longing for her old flame? It seemed so far-fetched. After all, Jimmy was a priest, and a dedicated one. What did Dennis have to worry about? Jimmy surely wasn't going to run off with Cindy. That wasn't in his character. He was truly a man of God.

Or maybe Dennis was greedy? With a wife who was relentless in her quest to have the most, to look the best, to drive the fanciest car and wear the nicest clothes … was that enough of a reason for Dennis to poison his long time client, Nancy, so he could get his commission from her estate now rather than wait until Nancy naturally died? Or maybe Dennis was innocent on all counts.

Kara knew she had to get some sleep. After reconfiguring the throw pillow under her head and adjusting the bed sheet and blanket, the ones she, thankfully, forgot to pack, she closed her eyes. Little Grey curled up next to her. "We need our rest, little friend. Let's go to sleep."

As if the tiny kitten understood, she closed her eyes too and was soon purring softly. It took Kara a bit longer to doze off. The scent of Old Spice lingered, even though Pa's favorite, oversized wing chair was gone. Now she wished she had kept it. To bring with her when she moved so she'd have it when Pa came for a visit. But if she did hold onto the chair, she realized in the next thought, how would she transport it in her Honda to Sue's, and then again to her new place, wherever that might be.

She lay there, staring at the once satiny pale gold draperies. She remembered the day her mother hung them. She walked into the house, home from fifth grade, and found her mother on a step stool, excitedly fastening each hook on the draperies to the extended curtain rod. They were one of the most luxurious and elegant things her parents ever owned. Kara remembered how giddy her mother felt when she came down from the step stool to admire them.

Now, decades later, they were faded from seasons of sunshine, limp from years of use. But even in their dilapidated condition, they still meant "home." A home she'd soon have to give up and an uncertain, slightly scary future she'd need to embrace.

Eventually, Kara fell asleep. What woke her up was the sound of Little Grey, filing her nails in the now nubby draperies. "Hey, you …" she groggily smiled.

The kitten turned to glance at her and, in the process, moved the draperies slightly apart. Apart enough for Kara to see, in the moonlight, that there was something square just outside her patio door. Her first thought was that Joe had left more cat food, or something related to cats. She knew he felt guilty that Little Grey had originated at his house and wriggled her way into Kara's heart.

Smiling, she got up from the floor and moved to the door. The moon made a spotlight on the brown wrapped box. It was too small to be cat food. Cautiously, she opened the door.

For a moment, her mind raced to the poisoned cupcakes that showed up at Twin Oaks. But this box wasn't from Vitale's bakery. It was brown, with no discerning identification. Kara stood at the door and gently opened it to find a neat stack of DVDs … all movies that starred Nancy Harding. "Girl On a Trapeze," "Beach Bodies," "Fun In the Sun" and "Lifeguards In Love." And a typed note attached. It said "See the resemblance?"

Kara had no idea who left them, or why. Was it Jack? But he would have brought them with him earlier. Maybe they came from someone who read her story about Nancy in the *Beacon,* saw her byline, and then found her address online. But leaving them at the back patio door, sometime in the middle of the night … that was odd, and slightly chilling. Then the note. "See the resemblance?" What did that mean? Resemblance to what?

Now wide awake, Kara made herself a cup of tea, then inserted one of the DVDs into her laptop and began to watch. But what she was looking for in the stack of Nancy Harding movies was beyond her.

The opening credits were silly, sexist really by today's standards, with a curvaceous cartoon character, supposed to be Nancy, frolicking with a beach ball as she pointed to each name … the director … the producer … the writer … throwing each of them, all men, an air kiss. Or, at least, that is what her sexy animated character was doing. Also listed in the credits was her co-star, Biff Daniels.

Kara couldn't watch more than a few minutes of each vacuous movie. One was more stupid than the other. All had the same plot. Innocent, gorgeous girl (Nancy) arrives for the

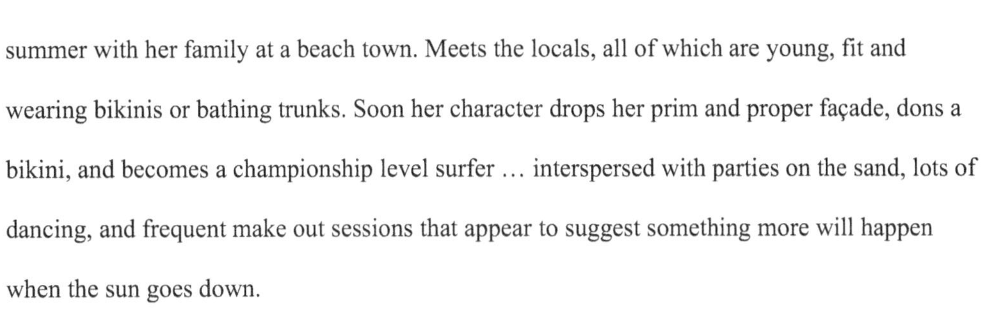

summer with her family at a beach town. Meets the locals, all of which are young, fit and wearing bikinis or bathing trunks. Soon her character drops her prim and proper façade, dons a bikini, and becomes a championship level surfer … interspersed with parties on the sand, lots of dancing, and frequent make out sessions that appear to suggest something more will happen when the sun goes down.

They were silly and stupid but apparently made Nancy, and Biff Daniels, verified Hollywood stars. By the time she reached the fourth movie, Kara was on her fifth cup of tea. The sun was rising. She glanced at the oven clock. It was six-oh-five and she'd had enough "fun in the sun" to last several lifetimes.

Chapter Thirty-two

"Jack? Did you leave those movies outside my patio door last night?" Kara knew Jack would be awake when she placed the call. He always was. But this morning, at six-ten, he actually sounded groggy, and annoyed, the way normal people do when they've been awakened at an ungodly hour.

"What?"

"You didn't leave me a stack of Nancy Harding movies? By my patio door? Last night?"

"No. What's this about?"

"I thought it was you. Now I'm confused. Anyway …"

"Anyway, go online and check out the sidebar. Front page."

Kara went to the *Beacon's* website. There, in the front page sidebar, was basically the tribute story about Jimmy that she proposed to Jack. It was titled "The Brother I Never Knew." Only it wasn't by her. It was by Jack, writing *her* story, as if HE were the one who was related to Jimmy. Where Kara wrote about Jimmy coming to her aid, Jack's version turned the tables and made HIM the hero, coming to Jimmy's aid. It was all a shameless pack of lies and Kara's first concern was for Jimmy's parents, that the Mullins wouldn't see it. To say she was angry would have been an understatement.

"Jack?! What on earth possessed you … WHY would you do that?! None of it is true. And Jimmy was MY brother!" She drew in a breath to steady herself, but the fury was still palpable in her voice. "And I thought we were holding off on any Jimmy Mullins stories until the police …" She paused. Her whole body was shaking. "What about Detective Cirelli?"

"Hey, I'm actually doin' you a favor. Until they catch Jimmy's killer, anyone who was close to him isn't safe. So now I'm the one his killer will come after." He paused, as if reading her mind. "I know. I know. Cirelli will be royally pissed at us."

"Not us. YOU!"

"Yeah, well, that's the chance I had to take."

"And you're willing to be Jimmy's killer's next victim? Just to protect me? If we waited a while and didn't go with my piece until after the police found Jimmy's killer, everyone would be happy."

"Yeah, well, they may never find Jimmy's killer. What with the Archdiocese not cooperating." He sighed, clearly frustrated with Kara for not seeing things from his perspective, which was always the way with Jack. "Anyway, it's a great story. People will eat it up. Newsstands will run out of copies. My publisher will be ecstatic."

"And Detective Cirelli will put you on his shit list."

"Hey, he's retiring soon anyway. Do I really care? And remember, if the *Beacon* stays in business, you'll get work."

Kara thought it presumptuous of Jack to believe that she wouldn't go elsewhere for a job. But he also knew how committed she was to the *Beacon* and what it, once, stood for.

"I'm very angry with you, Jack."

"You'll get over it. You think I'm cute."

"I … what?" she heard herself stutter.

"I know how you look at me. You think I'm handsome." It was so out of character for Jack to talk this way. In fact, it was totally weird and made Kara wonder if he had started to indulge in hallucinogenic drugs.

"Jack, you're a good guy … when you want to be. And the best editor I've ever known …" she said, realizing that he was actually the ONLY editor she'd ever known. "But you're dead wrong if you think my friendship and loyalty to you is based on anything other than that … friendship and loyalty … nothing more. Besides, you're not my type." Her thoughts went immediately to Joe.

"Well, if that's what you need to tell yourself. Anyway, this sidebar is gonna keep us in business. Mark my words. I'm waitin' for a call from the publisher. If our circulation bumps up as a result of today's issue, which it will, I can talk to him about hirin' you full time."

"Based on what? You stole my idea. How are you going to sell me?"

"Leave it to me, Fitz. Leave it to me."

Chapter Thirty-three

Kara ended the call, still shaking from anger and Jack's ridiculous insertion that she somehow harbored a crush on him. It was so unlike his usual gruff character to even approach the idea. What was going on with him?

She pulled the clothes she planned to wear that day out of a packing box … jeans, a T-shirt and a rose colored cardigan. The phone buzzed again. Six-twenty-eight. It could only be Jack.

"What did you forget?"

"When are you movin'?"

"How did you know I was moving?"

"You must've told me. Or I overheard it at the wake … or the funeral? I don't know."

"What? Does it matter when I'm moving?"

"I need to know where to mail your check."

"You can direct deposit it into my account at TD Bank."

"Nah … I don't trust that online banking stuff." It was true. Jack was the only person from her generation who literally hated technology of any kind. If he had his way, he'd still be using a Smith Corona and carbon paper to write his articles. Kara remembered how he kicked and screamed when he got his first laptop. It wasn't that he hadn't used a computer for school papers and assignments. It's just that he never liked them.

"Well, I'm moving to Sue Butler's cottage on her property at the Country Estates."

"Butler? The woman you were with at the wake?"

"Yes. You have a pen handy? I'll give you the address now." She knew better than to ask him to put her new address in his phone. He wouldn't know how to. "I should be moving there later today. One more night sleeping on old wall-to-wall will wreak havoc on my poor back."

"Country Estates. Not a bad address."

"You can send the check in Sue Butler's care. That way we won't confuse the mailman. Oh, wait, I don't think she's divorced yet. Better send it in care of Sue Butler Billings."

"You sure? I mean, she won't get pissed by my using her marriage name?"

"Well, I believe she is still officially married so, I guess either name, Butler or Billings, should be fine."

It was rare for Jack to be so persnickety about someone's exact name, but Kara was learning that there were several things about Jack's character that she never knew before.

Chapter Thirty-four

By mid-morning, Kara was nearly finished moving packed boxes into the trunk and back seat of her Honda. Soon it was clear that she'd need to make two trips to the storage facility. After that, she'd stop at Twin Oaks to see Pa. She figured by late afternoon, probably at dusk, she'd finally arrive at the Country Estates. That was the plan. Then Joe called. She smiled when she saw his name on her caller I.D.

"Hey, I've got some time today. Do you need any help packing up? Moving? I've got my truck."

"That's so thoughtful, but I'm okay. Most of the boxes are already over at the storage facility. I've just got two more trips. But thanks."

"How was sleeping last night? Any aches and pains?"

"It was fine, but I don't think I can handle another night roughing it." She stopped short of telling him about the Nancy Harding films. If Joe was the person who sent them, he would have asked how she liked them. But he didn't.

"Listen, Kara, I was thinking … and I know it's none of my business. But you said your friend is going through a divorce."

"Yes, she is. That's why she wants me to move into her cottage as soon as possible. Before her husband … her estranged husband does."

"It's just that … well … divorces can get nasty. I know."

She was taken off guard. "Joe, were you once married?"

"Long time ago. We were kids. We weren't married long. But even though we remained cool with each other, it was still hard once the lawyers got involved. Are you sure you'll be okay living there?"

"Umm … yes," she answered quickly before she could think about his question. She had no alternative. At least not now. She *had* to move into Sue's cottage. Or was Joe trying to frighten her in the hope that she'd move into his place? She didn't know him well enough to know his motives. "It's only for a short time."

"Well, if you change your mind …"

"I'll be fine," she answered confidently. "Oh, by the way … did you drop off a stack of DVD's last night? At my patio door?" She figured there was no harm in asking.

He hesitated. "No. Why?"

"Nothing." She paused. "Well, we'll stay in touch."

"Definitely. I've got your address. I've got your number."

She could tell that he was sorry about her move. She was too. But she had no choice. The house was as good as sold. The closing was now only a week away. She had to get out. And she had to get to the cottage before Sue found someone else to occupy it.

She made another cup of tea before she packed up the kettle. The phone rang again. It was Joe … again. "Hey, I was thinking about what you said … about the stack of DVDs someone left on your patio. Was there a note or anything with them?"

"A note but no name. It said, 'See the resemblance?'"

"Huh?"

"I know. Weird, right?"

"Resemblance to what? What kind of movies were they?"

"All Nancy Harding films. I suspect they were from someone who caught my byline on the story about Nancy in the *Beacon*."

"Maybe. But what do they mean by resemblance?'

"Have you seen any of her films?"

Joe hesitated. "Yeah. On TCM. As a kid. Late at night. Usually when I was up with a bad cold. Stupid, lightweight stuff."

"Yep," Kara said, trying to dispel his obvious concern. But now, in thinking it through, she was beginning to wonder who would have the audacity to walk onto her property, come around to the back patio door in the middle of the night and leave the DVDs with such a cryptic question.

"You know, Kara, thinking about it … you kinda DO look a little like her. Nancy, I mean. Same features. Same build." He then joked, "And all this time you didn't know you could've been a movie star!"

"Uh … thank you but I don't think I'd quite fill out a bikini like she did," Kara joked, then blushed at her own forwardness. She didn't want Joe to think she was flirting. Not yet.

"I'm sure you'd do any swimsuit justice," he countered, sounding more serious than silly in his reply. Kara felt herself blush. Again.

"Well," she continued awkwardly, "I'd better get going."

“Will you call me when you get settled? Just to touch base?”

“Yes. If you want me to,” she promised, feeling for the first time in a very long time that someone, other than her parents, really cared.

Chapter Thirty-five

Kara called Sue from the car to tell her she'd be arriving later today.

"Oh …" Sue's tone put Kara on guard.

"Is there a problem?"

"No, no. It's just that Steve is coming around to pick up some things. I won't be here. If he sees you moving into the cottage, it might set him off." She paused.

"I thought you wanted someone in there so he wouldn't move in himself."

"That was the plan. But now, if he sees you in the process of moving … well, I think it would be better if it were a fait accompli."

"So are you saying tomorrow is better?"

"Yes. Tomorrow would be great."

Kara finished the call and sighed. Little Grey, as if sensing her mood, hopped onto the kitchen counter and rubbed against her arm. "You disappointed too?"

She caressed the tiny cat's fur, then glanced into the living room where the bare, stained avocado carpeting awaited to provide another night of restless sleep.

With her plans changed, Kara needed food to hold her over until tomorrow. So much for a spotlessly clean fridge. Milk. A sandwich from the deli for dinner. Thank goodness she hadn't yet packed away the teabags, kettle and her favorite cup. Not to mention Little Grey's bowl and a few cans of Fanci Feast.

The rest of the morning and early afternoon were spent carting the two remaining boxes over to the storage facility. By mid-afternoon, she pulled a fresh sweater and jeans from the clothes she already packed to take to the cottage, showered with the one towel she hadn't yet packed away, and set off to see Pa.

A thick cloud cover moved in. If she hurried, she would get to Twin Oaks before the rain came. If she got caught in the deluge, she might miss visiting hours. Twin Oaks had a strict policy about not allowing any visitors into the dining room during dinner.

Chapter Thirty-six

The drive was tense. Her knuckles turned white on the steering wheel as the rain dumped buckets onto the sunroof of the Honda. Kara slowed down whenever she approached a swath of wet leaves on the asphalt. Slippery devils, she thought. At one point, she pulled over, thinking a black sedan was following her. But when she glanced back through her rearview mirror, the car was gone.

The rain continued to pound relentlessly. It switched direction rapidly and was now banging against the passenger's side door. Kara hated driving in storms, especially this kind. Wild and ferocious. And so she waited, Impatiently. Until the rain subsided and the coast was clear.

She checked her phone. It was almost five o'clock. Was she going to miss her chance to see Pa today? Had she come out in this horrendous storm for nothing? Then the phone buzzed, causing her to nearly jump out of her seat. It was Jack.

"Hey … what's up?"

"Jack, I'm sitting on the side of the road, about half a mile from Twin Oaks, waiting for this damned storm to move on so I can see my Pa before visiting hours are over … what is it?"

"Okay. Okay. I'll be quick. While you're there, can you stop by that director's office and see if you can find a copy of Harding's will?"

"Jack, we already discussed this. She told the police that she didn't have a copy of the will."

"I think she's got a copy. She cleaned out Harding's room. You mean to say she didn't come across the will?"

"Again, even if she does have it … why would she just hand over Nancy's will to *me*?" She stopped, suddenly realizing what Jack was asking of her. "No, Jack. I'm not going to sneak into the woman's office to look for it."

"You can say you want to talk with her about your father. See how he's been settling in." Then he asked, "You gonna be there in, say, an hour?"

"If the rain subsides, I should be there in half an hour. Why?"

"I'll call her office in an hour. That should give you enough time."

"Time for what?"

"I'll tell the secretary that I need to speak with the director, immediately, about my father who's dying and wants to put Twin Oaks in his will. You can bet the secretary will interrupt your meeting. That director will leave her office to take the call. That's when you start looking around her desk for Harding's will."

"That's crazy, Jack. What if she catches me?"

"Just tell her you lost an earring and thought it bounced onto her desk."

"Wow, you're devious."

"I need that will."

"Oh, I see. You want to give it to Cirelli. Get back on his good side."

"Kind of like that. I heard from my contact at the precinct …"

"That cute rookie?" Kara teased. "The one you said was flirting with you?"

"Yeah, well," Kara could tell she embarrassed him. "Listen, just see if you can get your hands on that will." Then he added, "It's our civic duty."

"How is it our civic duty?" she chuckled.

"My contact at the precinct said Cirelli can't get in touch with Gregson. Gregson and the wife were supposed to be back from Spring Lake but never returned. Nobody at his office knows where they are. Gregson's got a copy of the will but he's avoidin' the cops." Then: "That's why I'm convinced that Gregson is protecting someone, or himself. Somewhere in that will is a clue to Harding's killer. I'm sure of it."

Kara wasn't fully convinced that Jack was dedicated to doing his "civic duty," but *could* imagine him publishing the will on the front page of the *Beacon* to boost circulation. And if Mrs. Warren was keeping a copy of the will from the police, that meant she was protecting someone. Possibly someone on her staff or a guest at Twin Oaks. Or possibly protecting herself.

She finished the call with Jack, just as the heavy rains subsided. Was that a sign? She wondered.

Chapter Thirty-seven

"How is my Pa doing?" Kara wasted no time. She was in Mrs. Warren's office. On a mission.

"Is there a reason for your question, Miss Fitzgerald?" Mrs. Warren said with concern. "I thought Daniel put your mind at ease. He told you that your father is doing quite well. No wanderings at night. Eating all meals. He's really a model guest." She paused. Kara glanced down at her phone. Jack would be calling in five minutes. "Now if you'd like to talk instead about your editor. I'd like you to please ask him to stop sending texts to me and my secretary about getting a copy of Nancy Harding's will. As I told Detective Cirelli, I never saw a will."

Kara shook her head. "I'm sorry. I'll talk with him."

"I'm still angry with how he broke the news about Nancy's poisoning. I can't tell you how many calls I got from our guests' worried family members.."

"I'm sorry about that."

"And as I said to the police, the only person who would have a copy of Nancy's will is Dennis Gregson."

"Yes. I understand from my sources that the police are still trying to track him down."

"I'm not surprised. He's a weak man. You can tell just by looking at him. I have no idea why Nancy kept him on as her accountant *and* executor. That wife of his … she was always flaunting herself. Her hair. Her figure. Her clothes. Her cars." Mrs. Warren looked off. "I suspect Nancy kept Gregson on because she didn't like losing people. She once told me that, when she was a young woman, she lost her family. Then she lost Biff … Daniels … the love of her life. He died in that motorcycle crash." Her voice trailed off. Then there was a knock at the door. Her assistant appeared.

"I'm sorry to interrupt, but I have a man on the phone. He says his father wants to leave Twin Oaks something in his will and he'd like to speak with you."

"Please take his name and number and tell him I'll get back to him shortly."

"I did that but apparently he's about to get into a private plane and will be tied up in meetings with his team for several hours en route to Bermuda."

Kara tried to hide the smirk on her face. Jack certainly had a vivid imagination.

"Excuse me, Miss Fitzgerald. I'm not sure how long this call will be."

"No problem. Do you mind if I make a private call myself? I tried earlier from my car but couldn't get a signal."

Mrs. Warren looked puzzled, but quickly recovered. "You want to use my landline?"

"Yes. If you don't mind."

Kara could tell that Mrs. Warren's nod did not match her true feelings. But she pointed to the phone with one of her well manicured fingertips, then left her office. Kara wasted no time slipping behind the desk. To keep up the ruse, she picked up the phone receiver and cradled it against her ear, keeping it in place with her shoulder as she got to work sifting through the ream of folders on the desk.

Her heart beating hard, she drew in a breath. Nothing. Nothing. Nothing. And then … buried beneath a pile, she saw a folder simply labelled "N. Harding." She opened it. Her heart pounding. Her breath stuck in her chest. Contracts. Agreements. Notes about Nancy's food preferences. A few antibiotics she needed during various illnesses. And then, under that stack, a "Last Will and Testament."

Kara slid the stapled papers out, folded them, and placed them in her purse. Then she replaced the folder in the stack, placed her purse over her shoulder, and moved smoothly out of the office, down the hall, and to her car.

Chapter Thirty-eight

The roads were slippery, covered in a wet carpet of thick gold and amber leaves. Kara drove quickly away from Twin Oaks, but careful to mind the slick, until she came to the main road. Her heart was still pounding. Would Mrs. Warren find out about the missing will today or tomorrow or the day after that? She would certainly think back to the moment Kara asked to use the phone in her office. But it didn't matter. Mrs. Warren was clearing hiding something in the will from the police, Kara was going to find out what that was. Jack, she reluctantly admitted to herself, was right.

After driving about a mile, she saw a Home Depot in the distance and pulled off the road and into the parking lot. There, she took Nancy Harding's will out of her purse and was about to skip through the pages in search of the section titled "Beneficiaries" but something stopped her. On the title page, under "Last Will and Testament of Nancy Harding" there was written in smaller font "a.k.a. Jane Jones."

Kara's heart nearly stopped. *Jane Jones*?! What were the chances that Nancy was THE Jane Jones? The woman who gave her and Jimmy up for adoption?

She drew in a breath. Then she leafed through the rest of the document. When she came to "Beneficiaries" she allowed her eyes to slide down the list. There were a few names listed, people who were to receive twenty-five thousand dollars each … Daniel, the orderly, was among them, along with the names of a few other people who Kara didn't know. Was this the reason why Mrs. Warren pretended not to have the will? Was she protecting Daniel, and others, from becoming suspects in Nancy's murder? Perhaps. But that still begged the question: Would any of these people kill for twenty-five thousand dollars? It was not chump change for sure. But it wasn't a king's ransom either. Not an amount of money worth going to prison for … for life.

In a separate paragraph Nancy listed Dennis Gregson, who she described as "my essential and loyal accountant and executor." Dennis was due to receive serious money, two million dollars. Now that kind of money would certainly come in handy for a weak man who was always trying to please his spendthrift wife. Under *that* paragraph was another notation. "I give the bulk of my estate to my four heirs."

Kara presumed that Ricky Wexner was one of the heirs, but who were the other three? And still, the burning question, was Nancy Harding the same person as Jane Jones … *the* Jane Jones who gave her and Jimmy up for adoption? Kara wasn't thinking about money for herself. Instead, the next thought that came to mind was, "is this what the person who sent the DVDs meant when they wrote 'see the resemblance?'"

And who were these four unnamed heirs? Certainly they were due to inherit a significant amount of money … even more than the two million that Dennis Gregson was going to get. No, we were talking big money here. And as Kara contemplated why Nancy had not actually listed the names of her "heirs" in her will, it never occurred to her that she herself might be one of them.

Chapter Forty

The phone buzzed. Kara was still in the car, staring at the will. "Well? Did you get it? Find anything?"

"Jack …" she paused. She was at a crossroads. "I found nothing."

"What do you mean *nothing*?"

Kara decided not to tell Jack about the will. It was a police matter. And in a way, she was protecting Jack from himself, from ruining his relationship with Detective Cirelli, the parental role model that Jack needed ever since John Logan died.

Kara knew that if Jack published the will, there'd be no more exclusives or inside information given to the Beacon. The police would never again trust him with any information. Not to mention that exposing the people who were set to inherit money from the estate could put their lives in jeopardy. Whoever killed Nancy clearly wanted to get their hands on all the money, and wanted to get rid of any competition for it.

It never dawned on her that, if she and Jimmy were the illegitimate children of Nancy Harding, or Jane Jones, they could have stood to inherit some of that money … which may have put Jimmy in danger. Which could now put her in danger too.

Kara knew her next stop had to be the police.

Chapter Forty-one

"Mrs. Warren clearly lied to you," Kara said as she handed Cirelli the will.

"Yes, she did. But I'll protect you if Mrs. Warren suspects you took it. Though as she was withholding evidence, I doubt she'll report it missing."

"There's one other thing," Kara hesitated. The detective raised his thick eyebrows. "I noticed on the front page that Nancy Harding wasn't her real name." Cirelli looked at the will.

"Jane Jones?" he said curiously. "I'm not surprised she changed her name. But that does change how we track down her heirs. That's why I need Gregson to give me the names of all the beneficiaries."

"There's something else," Kara suddenly felt silly. There was no proof that the Jane Jones who gave her and Jimmy up for adoption was the same Jane Jones who became Nancy Harding. Still, it was a strange coincidence. "Jimmy and I were put up for adoption by a Jane Jones." She then watched as Cirelli blanched.

"Oh …" was all Cirelli said. But Kara knew he was taken aback. "Let me handle this," was all he said, but Kara knew that what was going on behind those four words was a full chapter going on in his mind. Still, she didn't think there was any reason for concern about her own safety. If Jimmy was murdered by a jealous priest, what did she have to worry about?

"Detective, you'll notice that Nancy didn't list her heirs … the people who will inherit the bulk of her estate."

"I see," he sifted through the pages. "We should know more soon. My guys tracked him and the wife down. They went from Spring Lake straight up to some fancy resort in Killington, Vermont. Told him there'd be a subpoena out for his arrest … evading law enforcement … if he didn't appear in my office pronto." He then added, as if comparing his own marriage to the Gregson's, "kind of feel sorry for the guy. Seems like a weak man to me, married to the wrong woman." Kara agreed with the detective about the odd coupling in the Gregson household, but kept her opinion to herself. "Oh, and Kara …"

"Yes?"

"When Gregson gives me the names of those four heirs Nancy mentions in her will, I'll of course know for sure, but until then, stay somewhere safe, okay?"

"I will … but I don't understand."

"Whoever killed Nancy and Jimmy wants all that money to him or her self. We'll keep a tight rein on Gregson and, now that we know who the heirs are … at least after he tells us … he'll know we're watching him."

"You mean that Jimmy was killed because he stood to inherit some of Nancy's money?"

Cirelli nodded. "We have a murderer out there who stands to inherit the entire estate. And for two people already to be killed for it, there must be a fortune in that estate." Kara felt her insides shiver. What the detective was telling her was that, if she was someone who Nancy considered an heir, then her own life was in danger. Cirelli sifted through the pages as if looking for a clue. "Kara, it says here there are four heirs. Wexner is probably one of them. Jimmy was most likely another. You. If my hunch is right. That leaves a fourth heir. Have any idea who that fourth heir would be?"

"Detective, I'm not even certain I'm one of them myself. But no, I have no idea."

"Well, until we have Gregson's input, and keep him a person of interest, you stay somewhere safe. Any friends you can bunk with for the time being?"

"I'm moving to a friend's cottage. Soon."

"Good. Don't tell anyone where it is, okay?" Kara instantly thought of how she had given her address to Joe. "And tell your friend to not tell anyone you're there. At least for now, okay?"

"Yes. Okay."

He then saw the fear in her face and tried to smile. "I'm sure you're fine but I'm a father and fathers tend to be overly cautious, especially with daughters. If you were my daughter I'd be telling you the same thing."

"I understand."

"Hopefully we'll get the names of all the heirs from Gregson. Soon. And maybe you're not on that list … which would be a good thing."

Yes, Kara thought to herself. Better to be poor than to be in fear for her life. And she smiled at the bitter irony. Then Kara thought of Jack's story in the *Beacon*, pretending to have been Jimmy's brother. Detective Cirelli clearly had not yet seen it.

"Detective, about Jack …" she drew in a breath, then told him about the stunt he pulled to boost circulation.

"Jack Logan better watch himself. He might have inadvertently set himself up to become the killer's next target." He sighed in frustration. "I'll call him. Tell him to lie low. If you're

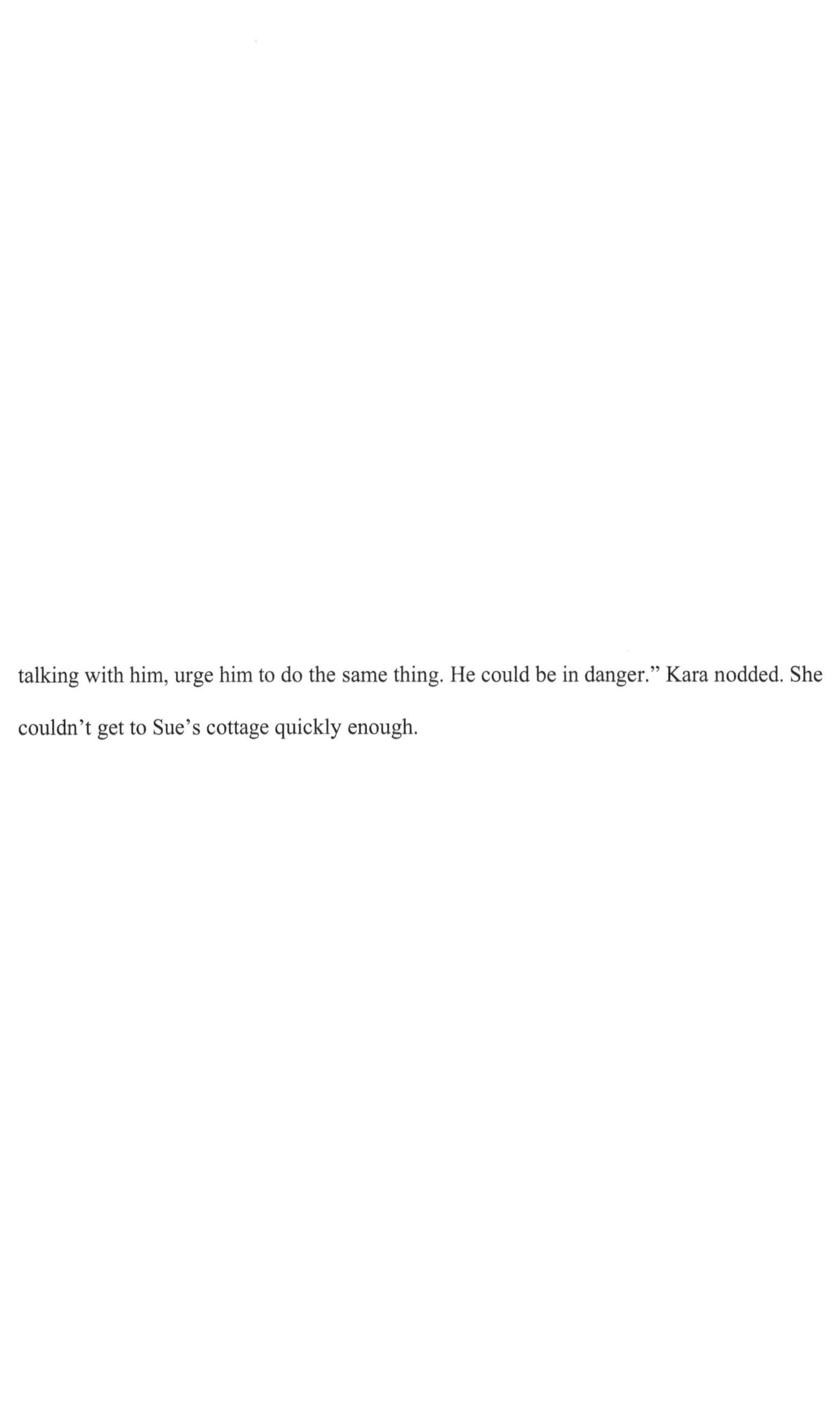

talking with him, urge him to do the same thing. He could be in danger." Kara nodded. She

couldn't get to Sue's cottage quickly enough.

Chapter Forty-two

Kara left the precinct, soberly contemplating her next move. She had to tell Sue that she might be in danger. Her only worry was that Sue would change her mind, not want to "invite" trouble. Up until this point, Sue, like everybody else, thought that there was no connection between Nancy Harding's murder and Jimmy's. But Kara had to take the risk of losing a place to live. It was the right thing to do.

Of course, it could be a coincidence. Dennis Gregson could identify Nancy's "heirs" as Ricky and three other people and that would be that. So Kara decided to lie low, to not say anything to Sue until she knew for sure. And as for the stack of Nancy Harding films? The ones that were left with the cryptic note "see the resemblance?" It could all be a weird mix-up. That someone read her story about Nancy being poisoned, checked out her photo next to her byline, and thought there were some similarities.

At least that is what Kara told herself to maintain her inner calm. She couldn't live in fear. And needed something to negate the negative feelings she was experiencing.

As she always did when faced with a personal crossroads, Kara decided to play a "Scarlett O'Hara." She'd worry about it tomorrow. Until then, it was time to move forward. To move to Sue's tomorrow and put every troubling, sad thought in the rearview mirror. She'd live in the cottage, find a job, close on the house and get on with her life.

When she got home, the sun was setting. On a whim, she saw the garbage cans on the side of the house. Tomorrow was garbage day. But there was a distant chance that the note that came with the DVDs will in there, probably stained by teabags and other debris, but still in tact.

And quite possibly, Kara could hand it over to the police for fingerprints. Just to put her mind at ease. That there was no malice involved in the gesture.

But two sweeps through the junk mail, lettuce shards, used paper towels and clumps of oatmeal revealed nothing. Besides, it was getting dark, and quiet. So she decided to go inside. After thoroughly washing her hands, Kara made sure, twice, that all the windows and doors were locked.

Without a TV or a book to read, as they were in storage, Kara made up the blankets on the carpet, facing the patio door. With a surrogated kitchen knife by her side, and Little Grey in the crook of her knees, she tried to close her eyes and get some sleep. It would be the last time she had to do this, she told herself. Tomorrow, she'd be at Sue's cottage, and no matter what condition the bed or futon or pull-out couch was in, it would be a far better sleeping experience. And what was worth smiling about.

Chapter Forty-three

Detective Cirelli was furious. Dennis Gregson had not shown up at the precinct and his secretary was giving the police the runaround.

"You tell your boss," he barked into the phone, "that I want the identities of all Nancy Harding's heirs within the next hour or he'll face obstruction of justice charges." He slammed down the phone. How dare that little weasel think he can evade a police investigation, Cirelli yelled to whoever was around the precinct. The secretary said he was "en route" from Vermont, but that didn't explain why Gregson wasn't answering his cell. He should have been in the precinct hours ago. Now it was nearly eleven p.m. and still no sign of him. What kind of game did he think he was playing?

Furious, he paced his office, then happened to notice that Bridget had slipped in at some point when he was distracted and left "dinner." He opened the brown bag, and then the foil-wrapped sandwich. Egg salad on a plain bagel, just the way he liked it. And a thermos of fresh coffee. "That's my girl," he instantly calmed down. Soon, he thought, he wouldn't have to deal with this nonsense anymore. He could get up when he wanted to, go to the Jersey Shore on a weekday to avoid the traffic to the beach, take in a matinee on Broadway … all the things he and Bridget talked about doing. Even take a cruise, he smiled. And with every bite of his egg salad sandwich, he could taste his retirement. It couldn't come soon enough … but not so soon that he was yet to solve the two murder cases on his lap.

Chapter Forty-four

Kara couldn't sleep.. Two nights in a row on old, smelly wall-to-wall was too much. Unable to get comfortable. She got up and switched on a lamp. The DVDs were still stacked on the kitchen counter. In the dim kitchen light, Kara glanced over the titles. They were silly … and embarrassing. "Dames and Dolls," "Beachy Bikini's," "Sand Blast. And she couldn't help but wonder, "was there really a resemblance between her and Nancy Harding?"

Not an obvious one. That was for sure. Nancy was gorgeous. Physically perfect. Her face. Her figure. But she couldn't deny that there was a suggestion of similarity. And if that was true, could she make the leap that Nancy and the Jane Jones who gave her up for adoption were, indeed, one and the same person?

On the cover of one film, Nancy posed with her real life lover, Biff Daniels. Biff was also anatomically perfect. Just like Nancy. But in studying his facial features, Kara couldn't help but see something of Jimmy in Biff's nose and chin. Even his hair was wavy like Jimmy's.

Which led her to wonder: Was Biff their father?

She pulled out her yearbook, the only thing she had not packed in storage as she wanted to go down memory lane with Sue when she got to the cottage. She thought it would be fun to remember happier times when Jimmy was alive.

She thumbed through the pages, finally arriving at the black and white photographs of Jimmy … taking a foul shot on the basketball court, supervising a fundraiser, joking with friends in the cafeteria. Yes, Jimmy did look like Biff Daniels. She wasn't imagining it.

Now wide awake and buoyed by a cup of Lipton's, Kara opened her laptop and searched for a biography of Biff Daniels. She found newspaper stories written after his untimely death from a motorcycle accident and, of course, his obituary.

It was a tragic death at a young age … thirty. Biff was not in Hollywood when it happened. Instead, he had driven his motorcycle to his sister's home in New Jersey's Watchung Mountains. That's where the brakes failed and he fell off a cliff.

As she read about the tragic scene, Kara felt her eyes tearing up. Was she actually reading about her birth father? The man whose DNA was inside her? And if Biff *was* her birth father, did he even know about her and Jimmy? Or had Nancy given them up at birth and Biff was none the wiser. And what about the other heir? There was Ricky, she presumed, and if the others included herself and Jimmy, was there someone else related to Nancy, an "heir," that only Dennis Gregson knew the identity of? Was this person also a "love child"? And, if so, did this mean that she still had a sibling out in the world somewhere? Or at least someone she was related to?.

Kara checked the kitchen clock. Three-fifteen. AM. Reading had made her eyes tired. Maybe she could get a few winks before dawn. Tomorrow or, rather, later today, was going to be a busy day. The day she'd finally move.

Switching off the lamp, she got back under the blanket, put her head on the pillow and, no sooner was she about to nod off when she thought she heard rattling at the patio door. At first she couldn't imagine she heard what she thought she heard. But then it happened again.

Kara's heart began to pump harder. She drew in a breath and glanced around for the knife she had earlier placed on the carpet next to her. But it was nowhere in sight.

A sudden downpour pelted the was vinyl siding. Perhaps a strong gust of wind was ratting the lock? she optimistically wondered. But then … again.

Bracing herself for … whatever … Kara rose to her feet, drew in a breath and, in the loudest voice she could muster, called out "Whoever is there I've got a gun!" The rattling stopped. Then a thump. Heavy footsteps against the patio pavers. Fading into the distance. Kara waited. And waited. When she didn't hear anything, and thought whoever was there was gone, she cautiously tiptoed into the kitchen, took the only remaining, unpacked knife … not the sharpest or largest but certainly better than nothing ….and approached the patio door.

Moving the draperies aside in one swift motion, she saw that the door was actually opened. Whoever had been there had gotten as far as successfully jimmying the lock to allow entrance. If she hadn't called out when she did, the intruder might have been successful.

Still, the question remained. Who was it? And why? What on earth was there in the house that was of any value? Unless that "value" was her.

She called the police straight away. An officer on duty said a patrol car would be stopping by immediately. Kara hoped, in the softened earth from the rain, that they might find a shoe print. Anything.

The police arrived five minutes later, long enough for any semblance of a footprint to wash away in the rain.

"Call a locksmith first thing," one of the officers, the female, commanded. "You got a baseball bat or something to put in the runner to jam it from opening?"

"I'll find something," Kara said hopefully. She had packed or given away almost everything. "And I'm moving tomorrow. I mean later today."

"Good. Don't give out your new address to anyone except those you think you can trust," the male officer suggested. "And get rid of that SOLD sign out front. Squatters look for that sort of thing. It's like an invitation to take over your space."

They left and promised to drive by throughout the rest of the night and to check the neighborhood for anyone exhibiting suspicious behavior.

Now alone, Kara, still shaken, sat in a corner of the living room, knife in hand, staring at the patio door until sunrise. She had placed a yardstick in the gulley to prevent the door from opening. And if the would-be intruder was a squatter, there'd be a new double lock on the patio door and the front door as well the next time they stopped by … if they dared. In the meantime, she'd count the days until she closed on the house, when it would no longer be her concern. And those days couldn't pass quickly enough.

Chapter Forty-five

As soon as the sun came up, Kara called a locksmith. Then she waited impatiently for three hours, for him to arrive. When he did appear, the fatherly old guy gave her an unnerving countdown of all the homes he'd been called to for lock changes after would-be "squatters" were caught casing the places.

Joe stopped by to check on Kara after a neighbor told him about the police presence the night before. "I wish you had called me. I would have stayed with you."

"It's fine. And I'll be at my friend's cottage tonight anyway."

"Well I can keep an eye on things tonight … make a few house checks before I turn in."

"Thanks, but I think these new locks and bolts should dissuade any possible intruders. Right Mr. Sansone?"

The elderly locksmith stopped what he was doing. "They will. But doesn't hurt to have a set of eyes on the place."

"And your address. At your friend's. Can I get it? I want to put it into my GPS." Kara's antennae were up. Detective Cirelli specifically told her not to share her new address with anyone. But was Joe really just "anyone?"

"Oh, uh …" she looked beyond Joe and could see the warning expression on Mr. Sansone's face. Then again, he and the detective didn't know Joe the way she did. And so she scribbled down the address to Sue's estate, hoping she wouldn't regret the impulse.

After Joe and the locksmith left, Kara wasted no time gathering up the remainder of her things, along with Little Grey in the cat carrier Joe loaned her, and packed up the Honda. The stress of the past few days was taking its toll. She couldn't drive to Sue's place fast enough. And, once she got there, her first order of business was to take a shower and a long nap. Then her phone buzzed. "Sue" read the caller I.D.

"I'm on my way."

"Finally!" She sighed. "Kara, just in case … I may not be there when you arrive. I've got to go out for a little while. But make yourself at home. Maria, my housekeeper, will have the key. Just ring the bell at the big house."

"I can't wait. I've had quite the experience … "

"Quite the what …?"

"Never mind, Sue. I'll fill you in when I get there."

Kara finished the call and smiled. A smile of relief. Whatever Sue's cottage looked like, it couldn't be worse than the anxiety and discomfort she was leaving behind. The place she once called "home" was no longer homey in her mind. It was time to move on.

Chapter Forty-six

Kara's compact sedan was packed to the gills. Hefty bags full of sweaters, jeans, jackets and her winter coat took up the back seat. There was barely enough room on the front floorboard for Little Grey's cat carrier.

"I just have one stop to make," she said to her tiny furry friend who looked as if she'd been sent to kitty prison by the expression on her face. "I know you hate being locked up, but I need to see my Pa. Then we'll get to the cottage and you can roam all around the place." She pulled out of the drive, turned right and proceeded to pick up speed as she neared the county road.

As she drove, Kara reminded herself about the missing will and figured Detective Cirelli was right about Mrs. Warren not mentioning it as she was as much to blame for lying to the police about having it in her files. And if she did mention it, Kara would of course play dumb. Still, it was puzzling that Mrs. Warren would hide it in the first place. What, or rather who, was she protecting?

The road began to meander through the rolling hills of acreage that led to Twin Oaks. Last night's heavy downpour had left the grounds mushy and leaf strewn. Soon there'd be no more leaves on the trees, Kara thought wistfully. She loved the beauty of autumn, but wasn't a fan of what came next … the harsh winds of winter. Then again, those naked branches would soon look like they were wearing coats of ermine once the first snow arrived. And that was the only reason she tolerated the season.

Now, as she drove, the barren trees allowed her to see Twin Oaks in the distance. Pa liked it here, she thought. It was a good move. Now all she needed was to find some peace and quiet for herself … and a steady job, hopefully at the *Beacon*. All the other intrusive thoughts, like whether Nancy Harding really was her birth mother, like what life would be like had she known Jimmy was her twin brother, and if she had another sibling somewhere in the world … all those thoughts had to be put on the back burner if she was going to get on with her life. God would reveal to her what she needed to know … at the right time. That is what her faith always taught her.

She parked the car, went inside, avoiding Mrs. Warren's office. She found Pa in the dining room with his new pals, holding court with his corny jokes. Kara didn't stay long. It was a simple visit. A pleasant one. And Kara was feeling good just seeing Pa feeling good. But, as she was leaving, a terrible thought came to her. Was Pa save here? As a matter of fact, was anyone safe here? It was not unheard of for killers to take innocent victims if only to take the police off their game.

The thought was a legitimate one and, hopefully, Twin Oaks was taking precautions. They couldn't afford to lose another "guest" to murder. But if Nancy and Jimmy's killer, or killers were still at large, then nobody was safe.

Kara fought back tears as she drove away. She tried to cheer herself up by playing some music on the radio, but nothing soothed her spirit. Then she reminded herself that she was going to a new "cottage," a place in a beautiful part of the state. And with that thought, she drove to her new life.

Chapter Forty-seven

Country air. Fresh and clean. A hint of hay. Earthy. Kara's spirit came to life. Pure nature had that effect on her.

She turned the car onto Downey Highway, a two lane rural road that served as the thoroughfare into and out of the Country Estates. According to the GPS, she was still twenty minutes away. Opening the sunroof, Kara drank in the elixir of a pristine autumn day. And she was the only car on the road. In fact, there was no civilization in sight until she spotted a small market. She needed a few things, like cat food and milk. That was about all she could afford as the check from the *Beacon* had not yet arrived in her account. The woman behind the counter looked surprised to have a customer.

Once back on the road, Kara drove several more miles, enjoying the peace and quiet. It was turning into a cloudy afternoon. A low front was settling in. Then, in her rearview, she caught sight of a black sedan gaining ground. As there were no other cars in sight, she expected the sedan would pass her by. But as it drew closer, she felt it breathing down her neck. If she stopped suddenly it would surely ram into her rear bumper.

She veered slightly onto the pebbled curb, allowing him to pass in their lane, but the sedan kept pace, swerving with her Honda as if it wanted to push her off the road and into the adjoining drainage ditch.

Kara could do nothing but drive. Faster. Faster. Until she saw what appeared to be a tiny church in the distance. Stone. A bronze cross on top. In a split second decision she made a sharp right, still at breakneck speed, rumbling onto the gravel drive and into the empty parking lot. She was shaking as she watched the black sedan barreling down the road. "Dear Lord, what was that all about?"

She wasn't sure if the car would turn around. It was definitely dead set on harassing her. For a few moments, she forced herself to take deep breaths. What, she wondered, was going on? Had she cut the driver off at some point? No, she told herself. She had not. And if he was in that much of a hurry, why didn't he just drive past her? He could easily overtake the initial speed she had been going.

Then a knock on the window. She jumped. "You alright?"

It was a man in his Forties wearing cleric's garb … all black with a white collar. He said he had seen the black sedan mowing her off the road from the window in his office at the church. After introducing himself as "Mr. Parker," he suggested Kara might want to come into his parsonage for a cup of tea.

"You should take a few minutes to catch your breath. My housekeeper always keeps crumb cake in the pantry."

Kara nodded. As she opened the car door, she suddenly became aware that Little Grey had been jolted off in her carrier upside down and was meowing loudly. "Bring your friend inside too."

"Thank you."

They sat in the kitchen of the tiny parsonage. Little Grey lapped up some milk. Kara sipped tea and gobbled up the best homemade crumb cake she'd ever tasted.

"Do you mind if I pray for your safety?"

"Not at all," Kara smiled and she bowed her head as the cleric requested God's protection over her, Little Grey and her car. When he finished, Kara felt slightly better.

"Did you catch the car's license plate?"

"No. It was too close. Nearly touching my bumper" She realized her hands were shaking.

"Just sit here as long as you like. The ladies from our church council will be arriving shortly so you won't be alone." Then he added, "I doubt that driver will dare come back once he gets a look at our council ladies. Together, they'd pack quite a wallop," Mr. Parker smiled, and Kara knew he was trying to help. "Do you have far to travel?"

"I'm on my way to a friend's home in the Country Estates."

"Country Estates? That isn't far." He then excused himself and Kara was alone but only for a few moments as she could hear the sound of cars on gravel outside. The church council women had arrived. Suddenly there were a dozen cars in the parking lot and just as many women milling about, Kara felt more secure enough to return to her Honda and get back on her way.

The road was once again empty, but she felt better as she drove. The sky was darkening, the way it goes grey and then deep blue before nightfall sets in. But she could still see. Acres upon acres suddenly appeared, a thick carpet of deep green, interspersed with hay bales, pumpkins in vast patches … comfort sights and sounds. Soon there were horses. Everywhere. Roaming the fields. Grazing beside their colts. All was well once more.

<h2 style="text-align:center">Chapter Forty-six</h2>

Kara lowered the window to enjoy the crisp fall breeze. She didn't have long to drive. Then her phone buzzed. It was Sue. Kara switched on the speaker.

"Where are you? I had hoped to see you before I had to leave."

"I think I'm close. The GPS says I should be there in fifteen minutes."

"Well, if I miss you, get the key from Maria." Then: "Did you hear about Dennis? Gregson?"

"No. What?"

"Cindy just called. He's being questioned by the police about Nancy Harding's murder." The news wasn't new to Kara. Dennis Gregson and Cindy had been evading the police and Kara figured Detective Cirelli finally pinned him down. "Do you really think he killed her?"

"I don't know, Sue. I guess as he's her executor and accountant … I don't know. I mean, at the very least, he stands to get something from Nancy Harding's estate … if only his cut for handling her business all these years."

"Still, it can't be that much. Don't you think?"

"Uh … I don't know." Kara suddenly saw the sign for "Country Estates" and turned right as instructed by the lady on the GPS. "Hey, I'm nearly at your place."

"Oh! Good! Well make yourself at home. I made sure Maria stocked the fridge."

"Sue … you didn't need …"

"Nonsense! Besides, if Steve sees the fridge full, he'll believe that I really do have a tenant living in the cottage."

"I can't thank you enough, Sue."

"My pleasure. Just get settled and maybe I'll see you later, okay?"

"Okay." Kara could see the dim lights of palatial homes in the distance … dots of gold amidst the black night. This was where she would live, she told herself as she smiled. This was going to be her new home. And already she felt like she belonged.

Chapter Forty-seven

Kara found herself on a long, stone paved drive. A sign that she could barely make out said "Private." As it was pitch black, she could just about see fields and, in the distance, the outline of a barn. To her left, about a quarter mile ahead, was a huge brick and stone house.

Back at the church, the Reverend Mr. Parker couldn't stop thinking about the young woman who was nearly pushed into a ditch by a wayward driver. He grew especially concerned when some of the church women said they had witnessed the ominous black sedan driving wildly in the distance and how it literally forced a smaller car off the road. "God kept that girl safe," one of the women said, referencing how Kara found refuge in the parking lot of a church.

That's when Mr. Parker decided to see if anything was caught on the security camera in front of the church. He had it installed last year as his parish was in a desolate area but never had reason to use it. Now he was checking the footage from half an hour ago.

As he reviewed the film on his phone, he could make out the dark sedan. He rewound it again, this time he could see Kara's Honda and how the sedan clearly was aiming to hit her into a ditch.

"Reverend, look," one of the church council ladies remarked over his shoulder. "See the plate? I can make out most of it."

He realized that there was a license plate visible enough to get the first three letters and last two numbers. Only one number was illegible. Immediately, he called it in to the police.

Chapter Forty-eight

The cobblestone pavers leading to Sue's enormous home was lush with fragrant wild flowers and the sweet scent of new mown hay. Kara couldn't believe her good fortune. This place was more than a home, it was, as the name suggested, a "country estate." Horses were grazing in the midnight blue draped pasture. A greenhouse reflected the remnants of an autumn sunset. Then she came upon the house … a magnificent red brick and stone mansion. She had arrived.

At first she was puzzled. If this was Sue's home, as the GPS said, then where was the cottage? The cobblestone drive circled around to the front entrance of the main house, and there was also a cobblestone driveway to the far right of the house. No cars. But a tiny light was twinkling in a small window set in the rear of the great house. That's when Kara realized that she was idling her car just a few feet away from … the cottage. A charming miniature of the main house. Only with French doors at the entry. A slate path leading to those doors. And terra cotta pots overflowing with brilliant yellow mums that were haloed by small patio lights.

"We're home," she smiled at Little Grey. She could hear water in the distance and followed a trail of patio lights that led down a small hill which in turn led to a gurgling brook. With Little Grey in her carrier, she stood on the bottom stone step and realized, in the twilight, that she was standing on the precipice of a small pond.

Suddenly she was overcome with gratitude and awe. Nothing could have prepared her for this. It was far more than she ever could have imagined. Then she remembered Sue saying that her housekeeper, Maria, had the key to the cottage. But Kara couldn't resist trying the French doors. Planters of yellow mums framed them. Patio lights welcomed her. The door opened. And then she felt the presence of someone approaching. She turned. In the soft light, she made out the frame of a tiny woman in a blue maid's uniform.

"You Meees Kara?" her voice was as gentle as her smile.

"Yes! And you must be Maria."

"Si. Meesus Sue say you come soon."

"Is Sue here?"

"No. She go out," Maria said softly. Kara couldn't help but notice a bronze Mercedes, Sue's Mercedes, sitting in an open garage behind the house.

"Oh … I'm sorry I missed her."

Maria was holding a platter covered in foil. "Thees I make for you. Cheekin. Roast. With potato?" The fragrant aroma reminded Kara that she hadn't eaten anything decent in days.

"Thank you. It smells delicious."

Kara put Little Grey's carrier down as she accepted the plate.

"I go home. To MY house. But I come back tomorrow. Mees Sue be back later. You be okay?"

"Yes. I'm sure I'll be fine. Thank you. Again."

Instead of returning to the house, Maria started to walk toward a van that was waiting for her at the end of the drive. Kara turned back toward the cottage, placed the food on the ground, and opened the door to enter.

"Oh, no, you don't," she playfully scolded Little Grey who was meowing at the aroma of garlic chicken. "We'll share."

One step into the cottage and Kara knew she was in a world that only existed, before now, in her dreams. Even in the dim light of a small lamp on the marble kitchen counter, Kara knew she was going to be extremely happy here.

She opened the cat carrier and Little Grey got to work exploring, but not going too far away from the plate of chicken. Kara broke off a tiny piece of meat. "That's for being such a good girl."

Now it was time to explore her new home. She turned around to take in the main floor. And though it was dark outside, the area was bathed in thin, azure blue … courtesy of a large skylight above the main space. It was a homey space. Kara gazed over the welcoming scene and nearly pinched herself. She was standing in an open galley-style kitchen. Marble countertops and a matching island. .Against the far wall, the wall with the white porcelain farm sink, was a huge window that stood three feet high and stretched four feet wide. It overlooked the wood surrounding the pond, which she could only imagine was a spectacular view in the daytime. Beneath the window and on either side of the farm sink were the appliances. Stainless. Including a wine cooler stocked with chardonnay and champagne. Above it a wine rack for the reds. Birch and glass cupboards housed Royal Worcester fine china and an array of Waterford crystal. In a main drawer beneath the farm sink was shiny silver cutlery along with a collection of carving knives. Everything a gourmet chef could want. "I should take up cooking!" Kara said to Little Grey. The stainless steel fridge was just as impressive with an array of healthy food including berries, lettuce, eggs, butter, whole grain toast and milk. Teabags, plenty of them, were in a cannister next to the sink.

Kara found a corkscrew in the utensil drawer and proceeded to open one of the chilled bottles of chardonnay, pouring an ample amount into one of the sparkling Waterford goblets. Then, glass in hand, she explored the rest of the cottage, switching on lamps as she moved about the place.

From her vantage in the main room, she could look up to the loft. There was a huge skylight above the sleeping quarters. It took up practically half the ceiling. Up there, Kara would, almost literally, be in heaven.

A cozy dining space adjoined the kitchen. A roughhewn oak table with ample room to seat eight. A milk glass chandelier with four tulip shaped lanterns. And on the table, a crystal vase stuffed with enormous blue hydrangeas.

To the left of the dining area was an enormous stone hearth. Surrounding it were three navy upholstered sofas, throw pillows in shades of taupe and cream, a thick taupe and cream area rug and, piled up alongside the hearth, a stack of cherrywood.

There was a small bathroom downstairs, all white porcelain. Beyond it rose a staircase leading straight up to the sleeping loft with the huge skylight. Kara took the stairs. At the top she found a door leading to an en suite bath complete with clawfoot tub, pedestal sink and a separate glass enclosed shower. The window alongside the tub faced the front of the house and offered a view of the barn and farmland. Kara couldn't wait for sunrise so she could take a bath with a view.

Everything in the cottage looked new. Kara wondered if a guest had ever even stayed there as it all felt so fresh.

With her short but satisfying tour complete, it was time to eat. She was starving, having subsisted on two cups of tea all day. The aroma of garlic chicken was beckoning.

As she nibbled on the small feast, lost in the joy of her newfound good fortune, Kara almost didn't hear the knock at the door.

Chapter Forty-nine

A man who identified himself as a minister at a local country church called into the precinct with a complaint about a car he caught on his parish's CCTV cameras. A dark sedan that nearly pushed another car into a ditch not far from his church. He said the driver of the other car, the one that was pushed off the road, was not physically harmed but was quite emotionally shaken. He also remarked that several of the ladies in his church, en route to church for a meeting, had passed the same car and said it was driving at breakneck speed, nearly pushing them into a ditch as well. The license plate was traced and the cop on the desk said it belonged to a "Jane Jones." But the registration expired five years ago, around the same time that the car was reported stolen from Twin Oaks.

The officer posted the information into the database to alert neighboring precincts. When one of the cops assigned to the Nancy Harding murder saw "Twin Oaks" in the report, she immediately alerted Detective Cirelli.

"Detective, wasn't 'Jane Jones' Nancy Harding's real name?"

"Yep. Sure was," he answered as he glanced down at the copy of the Harding will that Kara Fitzgerald dropped off. This case, he thought, was getting stranger and stranger. Who would steal Nancy's car, keep it out of sight for five years, then drive like a bat outta hell along a basically deserted highway, pushing every other car out of its path? Who was the driver and where was he, or she, rushing to when they could easily pass any car by moving into the empty opposite lane?

But no sooner did Cirelli ask himself the question than he immediately knew the answer.

Chapter Fifty

While Little Grey got acquainted with the cottage, Kara grabbed one of the shawls folded near the hearth and took her glass of wine outside to sit on the flagstone steps leading to the brook and adjoining pond. It was now almost fully dark. The evening chill had settled in.

She was so grateful that she found herself thanking God, and looking forward to thanking Sue. And then, as if on cue, she heard the rustle of feet rummaging through fallen leaves coming from behind. When she turned, Sue appeared out of the night. She was dressed casually but expensively in designer jeans, a classic white turtleneck and a long white sweater. Her makeup, as always, was flawless and her hair pulled into a chic ponytail. She had her own glass of wine.

"You're here! Finally!"

"Sue, how can I ever thank you? This place is amazing."

"I thought you'd like it."

"I love it!"

"Come. I want to show you where I like to sit and think."

With the aid of low lights that lined the stone ledges leading to the pond, Sue guided Kara down a few more steps to a flat rock. It was just wide enough to seat two and offered a full view, even in the dark, of the pond.

"Here's to you." Sue raised her glass.

"To me?"

"Yes."

"But ... what did I do?"

Sue suddenly lowered her eyes. "Well, it's not really what you did. It's ..." she was searching, "you've taken it all so well. I mean ... losing your brother and all ..."

Kara did a mental double take. "You knew that Jimmy was my brother?"

"Well, everyone did."

"Everyone?"

"At Nelligan. I mean, Jimmy told Cindy and Cindy told the rest of us. I thought you knew."

"No. I just learned. Very recently." She paused. "After he died."

"Oh ..."

"Is that why you offered me your cottage, Sue? Because you felt sorry for me?"

Sue was quiet, then, "Well ... yes. But only after you said you were looking for a place. Is that so wrong?"

"No. It was very kind of you."

"And I wanted you to have those DVD's."

"You were the one who left them outside my patio door?"

"Well, I had someone drop them off."

"But you didn't sign the note. You should have let me know you sent them. It was very thoughtful." Kara was putting the pieces together. Not only did Sue know that she and Jimmy were twins, but it appeared that she also knew that they were the illegitimate children of Nancy Harding. "So, if you knew that Nancy Harding was my … Jimmy's and my mother …" she paused to capture the right words … "Did Cindy tell you that as well?"

"Yes. But Jimmy didn't know that part. Cindy only learned it later, after she married Dennis." Sue paused. "You had no idea that Nancy Harding was your birth mother?"

"Not a clue … until I did some investigating. Just recently. When I found a note that she wrote to Jimmy and me among my mother's things when I was packing up the house for the sale. She signed it with her real name. Jane Jones."

"And you found out that Jane Jones was Nancy Harding," Sue answered her own question.

"Yes." Kara suddenly felt as if she were undressed, naked and powerless. Sue clearly had known about her true identity for a while. Was the offer of the cottage only because she now thought Kara was "worthy" to live near her? No longer the shy, quiet, middleclass girl she was at Nelligan?

Sue turned to look at her. Directly. Actually, Kara was studying her. Staring. As if trying to determine if Kara was worthy of being part of her inner circle now that she was related to a former movie star. "You know, you *do* look a bit like her."

"Thank you."

"Yes. You have her eyes. And lips."

I wish I had her boobs!" Kara joked to lighten her discomfort. "But seriously, I wish I had known her." Then she smiled. "Sue, please don't stare at me. I'm not used to it."

"Sorry." She paused, looking back at the pond. "Then again, you were never the type to seek attention." It sounded like a back handed compliment. Kara let it go. She was, after all, Sue's guest in an incredible place and, under the circumstances, she couldn't afford to offend her. . "C'mon … let's toast to your mother. To Nancy."

Kara raised her glass to toast the woman she never knew but in whose body she grew for nine months. Who gave her life but not love. Who gave her looks but nothing else except the chance to be raised by two incredibly good people. And for that she toasted Nancy Harding. Then, suddenly, Sue rose from the rock.

"Well, I'm calling it a night. I've got an early start tomorrow. Meetings with my lawyer. Goodnight, Kara."

"Good night, Sue. And again, thank you."

"No need to thank me again, Kara. It's my pleasure. Believe me." Then she walked back to the main house.

It was only then, when Kara turned, that she noticed the dark sedan parked in the driveway. It was a distance back so she couldn't fully make out its color. Was it Sue's husband's car? She could only chalk it up to coincidence, still shaken from the near catastrophe she dodged hours earlier. Still, just the sight of a similar car sent shivers up her spine.

It was time to go inside herself. The temperature was dropping. She would make a fire with the cherrywood, heat up the kettle for a nice cup of tea, and settle in for a good night's sleep in a sumptuous bed under the star-studded skylight.

She had only walked a few steps toward the cottage when her phone buzzed. The caller I.D. said "Joe."

"How's it going?"

"Well, I was just sitting beside a lovely pond and listening to the sounds of nature."

There was a pause on Joe's end. "You don't sound like yourself, Kara. What's wrong?"

She stood outside the cottage door and told Joe what Sue shared with her. "Joe, I just learned that several girls from high school, one of them the woman who owns this cottage … they all knew who my real mother was."

He was quiet. Kara sensed he was gathering his thoughts. "Kara, who *was* your real mother?"

"Nancy Harding."

"The actress who just died?"

"She was poisoned. The police still haven't found her killer. And that other case. About Father Mullins. I recently learned he was my twin brother and he was also murdered."

"Kara, whatever is going on, you need to make sure you're safe. When we get off this call, lock all the doors. Close the windows." He paused. "I don't want to worry you. I'm sure you're safe. But just to be cautious, okay?"

"Yes. Okay."

"Good. I'm gonna hang up now. You call the police if you suspect anything. Promise me."

"I promise."

"And turn off your cell phone. That way nobody can trace where you are."

"I will."

He paused, then: "Sure you don't want me to come over and stay tonight?"

Kara knew Joe's intentions were honorable, but she didn't want to start a relationship this way. She didn't want him to see her as a victim, vulnerable. So she politely declined his offer and hung up, turning off her phone as Joe suggested. Then she went inside and locked the French doors behind her. So much, she thought, for a peaceful night's sleep.

Chapter Fifty-one

Whenever she felt uneasy, Kara's go-to remedy was a hot cup of Lipton's with a splash of milk. She filled the pristinely white kettle and set it on the stove. Then she took a white China cup out of the cupboard.

What Joe said, about being careful in light of Nancy and Jimmy's murders, troubled her. While she knew she had to be cautious, hearing it from him made her uneasy, especially about bringing harm to Sue. Had she inadvertently led a killer here? She only told Joe where she was. But did Sue carelessly mention it to Cindy … and Cindy to Dennis?

One good thing was that the police were keeping an eye on Dennis Gregson. That thought put her at ease. If he did kill Nancy and Jimmy to get access to the bulk of Nancy's estate, and was gunning for her, he had the eyes of the law squarely on him. Most likely, he'd lie low.

Drawing in a deep breath, Kara tried to soothe her nerves, a difficult task due to lack of sleep from two nights on dirty wall-to-wall.

She told herself that she was locked in, and could relax, at least for tonight. So she changed into comfy sweats, then cuddled up on one of the sofas in front of the hearth with a large cup of tea. Right now, all she could do was stay put, and wait until morning. Things would look much better in the morning. At least that's what she told herself.

Chapter Fifty-two

With the sound of the crackling fire in the hearth and the emotion of the past few days, Kara closed her eyes and came perilously close to dozing off. That's when she heard it. The persistent tapping on the French doors. In the half awake, half asleep zone, she took a moment to collect her bearings.

At first she thought it might be Sue, coming to check on her. But at closer glance, she realized it was Jack. She didn't know how he got there, but was immensely relieved to see a familiar face

"Jack!"

"I came to see how you're doing."

"How did you find me?"

"Your cell. When I saw you moved out, I traced you through the phone."

"Jack, you were worried about me."

He seemed to be looking past her. "Yeah."

"I'm glad you're here. I was thinking of some ideas for my next assignment …"

"Can I come in?"

"Of course! Wait till you see this place."

At closer range, Kara could see that he had a strange cast in his eyes. Jack had always been an "odd duck" as Pa would put it, but he was acting even odder than she was used to. His eyes began to dart back and forth. His hands began to fidget with something in his pocket. He wasn't looking directly at her.

"Can I get you some tea? A glass of wine?"

"No …" he moved in slowly, closer, closer. Kara backed up. She'd never seen Jack like this before. He was suddenly aggressive … and she wondered for a split second if he was coming on to her.

"Jack? What's on your mind?" She stepped back toward the wine cooler to gain some ground but he moved in to fill any void was between them. This was a different, and slightly scary side of Jack. Did he think his behavior was going to win over her heart? She had to let him down softly.

Then he blurted out: "She left ME for you and HIM."

"Who? Who left you?"

"Our mother dearest. Jane Jones. Known to the world as Nancy Harding."

"Jack?" she suddenly found the missing piece of the puzzle. Her mind was racing faster than her words. Then: "Jack, you are my brother?" She saw clearly what had been trying to come to the surface of her thoughts. There was always something in Jack that made her feel as if she knew him, though she, and others, thought him strange. Now she was learning that she, Jimmy and Jack were cut from the same cloth. But while she and Jimmy were woven smoothly, Jack was cobbled from remnants. A damaged soul. The anger he festered toward the world was pouring out of him.

"HALF brother." He glanced off, as if looking at something behind her. "That doesn't count."

"Of course it counts."

"She left me. She left me that day she drove off with that Biff good-for-nothing. Said she was coming back. But that was another lie. Lies. Lies. Lies." His blue eyes were black. "Who does that to a three year old?"

"Oh, Jack. I'm so sorry." She paused. "But she left Jimmy and me too." He wasn't responding. Something told her to get him talking. She had to bring him back to earth. He was drifting. "Talk to me about it. You must have been terrified."

He waited a long moment as if processing what she asked. Then: "She just walked away! Left me in a one room apartment. For God knows how long. Days. A week? Cops found me. Alone. Starving. Dehydrated. Sitting in my own shit. A baby. What kind of woman does that to her own child?"

"Who found you?" Kara couldn't imagine how anyone could do such a thing. Her heart was breaking for the baby who was clearly abandoned.

"Cirelli. He was on the force. Brought me home until foster care came. John Logan was on the force too. He was Cirelli's friend. They talked to a judge. Arranged for me to be adopted."

"By the Logans." She saw his hands fidgeting again with something in his pocket. Then he removed it. A crevat. Kara felt her entire body stiffen with fear. Was he planning to strangle himself? Right in front of her?

"Jack …" she said in the calmest voice she could muster. "Jane Jones didn't want me or Jimmy either. We were rejected too. You aren't alone."

He wasn't listening. Kara could tell he had a plan and it wasn't a good one. If she could only get through to him, she thought, reach him on some level before there was a tragic outcome.

"Jack … I care about you. And whatever you might think, you and I … we're all we have left. We are family."

He wasn't listening. His feet began to inch closer. Kara then realized that the crevat was not meant for him. She glanced around to get her bearings. She was in the kitchen, trapped between counters. Her first thought was to grab a knife to defend herself, but she couldn't remember which of the drawers held the cutlery. All she could do was move. Tiny steps. Move away from him as he drew closer.

"Jack? Is it the money from the will? I don't want it. You can have it all. Just don't do something you'll regret."

"It's too late now." He methodically pulled the crevat into position and moved in for the kill. Then …

It was Sue. At the French doors. Kara gasped. "Sue!" Sue put a key in the lock and entered. Just seeing her stopped Jack in his tracks. "Sue! Call the police. Now!" Kara screamed. But Sue wasn't moving. In fact, she stood in the galley kitchen, cutting Kara off, blocking her from leaving the area. Giving Jack a free hand.

"Do it, you idiot! Do it now!" Sue screamed at Jack who seemed frozen in conflict. Kara knew she had to do something fast, to use the element of surprise to break free. If she could get past them and into her car. She eyed her keys. They were back with her overnight bag, about six feet away, in the dining area … and she'd have to get past Jack to retrieve them.

"Do it! I'm sick and tired of you stalling."

Jack looked like a sick puppy … beaten down, controlled by a woman who had clearly used his fragile heart to her advantage. Kara saw the glazed look come over his eyes and darted under his arm, into the dining area. But before she could grab the keys and run, he spun around, now mentally awakened by Sue's verbal lashing, and began to position the crevat around Kara's neck.

Kara felt the strip of wire cut against her skin. She was able to get one arm free and tried to insert a finger into Jack's eyes. Her nails cut his cheek in the process. He winced but kept up the assault. And then …

"Drop it!" The voice was familiar. "Drop it before I shoot, Jack!" It was Detective Cirelli. He and two officers had bolted through the door, taking Sue off guard, and were holding her as Cirelli kept his gun firmly on Jack. "Jack, you don't want to do this." Then: "Let her go. We've got your girlfriend. It's over."

In the split second it took for Jack to consider Cirelli's words, one of Cirelli's officers crouched down and slipped behind him without Jack realizing it. In one swift move, he disarmed him from behind. The martial arts move took Jack by surprise and forced him to release the crevat. Kara began to cough, nearly choking before she could catch a breath. When she looked up, she saw the same officer and Detective Cirelli handcuffing Jack and leading him out to the squad car where Sue was handcuffed in a separate police vehicle.

"Get your things, Kara. You're going to stay with Mrs. Cirelli and me tonight." Kara, still stunned, followed Detective Cirelli's orders as she grabbed her purse and looked for Little Grey, who she found hiding behind the sofa. "Smart girl," she said as she placed the tiny kitten into the cat carrier.

"We can get that bruise on your neck checked at the hospital."

"It's okay, Detective. I'll put some ointment on it." She paused. "And if you don't mind, I'd like to stay at my house tonight. I still own it for the next few days."

"Your call, Kara. I can have my officers check the house throughout the night. Though you won't have anything to worry about. We cleared Gregson and his wife. We've got our murderers."

Murderers. The word hung in Kara's heart as she packed Little Grey and her clothes back into the Honda and drove "home." It was a sad ending to Jack's sad life. But there was nothing she could do for her half brother. He had made his choice, based on his personal insecurities. He had been used by Sue Butler to kill two people. In addition, Detective Cirelli said they were now going to reopen the Biff Daniels case. He said Jack was in the back of the patrol car bragging to one of the officers how he "bumped off" the actor by sabotaging the wheels on his motorcycle, causing the crash that took Biff's life.

Hearing it, Kara felt a shiver ride up her spine. That meant that Jack would be charged with three counts of murder. Surely he was looking at a lifetime behind bars. Sue, she presumed, would be charged with conspiracy in Nancy and Jimmy's murders. That would probably land her in jail for at least twenty years.

Chapter Fifty-three

Kara drove back to the empty house and slept better that night on the old wall-to-wall than she had in days. She was safe.

The following morning, Detective Cirelli stopped by. He said Jack told the police everything … how Sue Butler Billings had suddenly appeared in his life. She showed up at the Beacon one day under the guise of planning a fund raiser and asking for Jack's help. She used him, Kara, knowing that he was one of the beneficiaries in Nancy Harding's will. But Jack still thinks she's in love with him.

"And Sue only cares about the money."

"Apparently her husband's business dealings went bust. She was about to lose her lifestyle and needed a new benefactor. But she couldn't wait for Nancy Harding to die and she wanted the entire estate … not just Jack's cut."

The detective continued. Apparently Sue was a harder nut for his detectives to crack. They interrogated her for only a few minutes before she asked for a lawyer who promptly told her to shut up. "But the evidence against her as a conspirator is there. The DA will be able to build a strong case."

"Sue knew that Jack could be manipulated," Kara shivered at the idea of a vulnerable young man being used like that.

"You're lucky, Kara. She would stop at nothing to get rid of anyone in her way. She set her sights on Ricky but he was lucky to be locked up in that rehab center. Jimmy was next. You were going to be the third victim and, once she got her hands on Jack's cut of the estate, it would only be a matter of time before she found a way to get rid of him. I'm convinced of it. The woman is a psychopath."

"And she preyed on Jack's anger at being abandoned as a baby."

"Yes. And his hatred for you and Jimmy. He always blamed Biff Daniels for taking his mother away. And as you and Jimmy were Biff's children …"

Kara gasped. It was as she suspected. Biff Daniels was her and Jimmy's father.

"What about Jack's father?"

"We don't know who he is. But it's not Biff. That we know for sure."

?But how did Jack get access to Nancy without her suspecting he was her son?"

"I think that was what solidified his anger. He actually posed as a water delivery man. You know how lax the security at Twin Oaks was before Nancy's murder. He was able to walk in and pretend to be delivering water. He said he even stopped by Nancy's room under with the excuse that he needed directions to the cafeteria. Apparently she seemed to recognize him, according to Jack, but rebuffed him. Told him to get lost. That was the trigger that pushed him over the edge. After that, he was putty in Sue's hands."

Then, with the delivery man cover, he was able to surveil Twin Oaks every day, looking for a way to get the poison to Nancy. He recognized Ricky Wexner delivering a bakery box from Vitale's one day He called the bakery, pretended he wanted to order the same thing that Ricky Wexner was ordering to send to his favorite actress, Nancy Harding, and the woman on the phone gladly gave up the information about Nancy's favorite cupcakes."

"But Ricky went back to Florida. To rehab."

"Yes, but after Ricky left town, Jack arranged to keep up the cupcake deliveries. The staff at Twin Oaks just figured Ricky was arranging for the cupcakes to come in his absence. Jack would have the bakery leave them outside after hours. They had some kind of arrangement with the homeless shelters and soup kitchens so leaving day old food outside wasn't an odd request."

"How did he pay for the cupcakes without being traced back to himself?"

"He used Ricky's account." Cirelli said. "He'd pick them up then use a syringe to insert the arsenic into each one. After returning them to the bakery box, he'd leave it on the front stoop at Twin Oaks for one of the staffers to find it in the morning. The typed card on the box had Nancy's name. It was logical to assume they were from Ricky. Ordered by phone."

Kara was stunned. "Taking three lives for money." It was beyond her comprehension. As hard as it had been for her financially, she couldn't imagine committing murder for any reason, much less for financial gain.

"Money is, was, Sue Butler's identity. It's all she ever wanted. Even her marriage went south because she basically put Steve Billings into bankruptcy with her spending sprees. Poor bastard."

"And Jack was so starved for affection, he'd do anything for Sue."

"I'm afraid so."

"But the Logans were good to him." Kara was trying to make sense of the nonsensical.

"They tried. But Jack was so damaged from his mother abandoning him, I don't think he was ever able to trust their love for him. But Sue … he knew how to manipulate the guy."

"Jack was her puppet."

"And Jimmy? How did they manage that?" Kara's heart ached for Jack's lost soul.

"Sue was the one who organized the marriage retreat. The other couples weren't having problems in their marriages but she talked Cindy and Roberta into going. Jimmy only went as a favor … he thought he was there to help them spiritually, minister to them."

"Sue set him up."

"Yes. And Sue was the one who invited him to join her that morning on a hike. Poor guy was just trying to be a sympathetic ear. But she never showed. She left the Hague mansion the night before without telling Jimmy. He was waiting on the trail for her. A sitting duck."

"And Jack was hiding on the trail?"

"Yep. Poor guy didn't stand a chance."

"Poor Jimmy."

"And it would have been poor YOU next if we got to you a minute later."

"But how did you know where to find me?"

"When my guys questioned Dennis Gregson, they eliminated him as a suspect immediately. Then another precinct sent word that a pastor at a little church on the outskirts of the County Estates called in the plate number for a reckless driver. It matched Nancy Harding's tags, but her registration was out of date. The car had been reported stolen five years ago. I knew Jack was abandoned by Nancy … Jane Jones … whatever she called herself. So I took a guess that he stole the car and was the driver. Cop's instinct, I guess. When I heard the words Country Estates I knew Sue Butler Billings lived there. And that you had mentioned you were moving into a friend's cottage in that area."

"So you guessed Jack and Sue were in cahoots."

"Thank God we got there in time."

"Yes," Kara sighed. "Thank God."

Chapter Fifty-five

When Mr. and Mrs. Mullins learned that their son's killer was found, and who he was, they were beyond words. To even conceive that their boy Jimmy had a half brother, and that he stabbed him to death, was stunning and saddened them into silence. But when they learned from Detective Cirelli that Jack Logan had his sights on Kara as his next victim, they wasted no time in insisting that she move in with them.

"… for as long as you like," Mr. Mullins said. "Now we are your family.":

Kara didn't need convincing. Being alone with her thoughts was not a good thing. And living with the Mullins would be the closest thing she could get to living with family. In essence, they were her aunt and uncle.

So she moved into their spare bedroom. But on the morning of the close, Kara returned to her house to make sure everything was ready, that she left nothing behind. To her delight, and surprise, she found Joe waiting for her, sitting in a patio chair.

"I hoped you'd stop by," he smiled. Kara had told Joe she was staying with the Mullins. They had been trading texts. In one of those messages, he told her how much he missed her, and wanted to spend more time with her. Seeing him made her realize she wanted the same. That was the first day of their courtship.

Joe would arrive at the Mullins every evening after work. They'd grab something to eat. Sometimes they'd see a movie. Sometimes they'd sit at Joe's place and talk. It was the pace and the way Kara liked it. After several weeks, she brought him to Twin Oaks to meet Pa. And that meeting couldn't have gone any better.

"I'd like to someday marry your daughter," Joe said during one of their visits. To which Pa replied, "Do you love her better than you love yourself?" Joe smiled. "I absolutely do," he answered. And that was good enough for Pa. It was good enough for the Mullins too. They had become like surrogate parents to Kara. Mr. Mullins in particular grilled Joe about his "intentions." Naturally, Joe passed the test with flying colors.

But Kara wasn't ready for the altar. Not yet. She was emotionally fragile. Losing Jimmy was bad enough, but Jack's betrayal was turning her heart inside out. He was, after all, her only living sibling. Once she tried to visit Jack in prison but he refused to see her. Hopefully, one day, he'd come around.

Chapter Fifty-five

It took a year to sort through Nancy Harding's estate. During this time, Kara was able to take on freelance writing assignments at the *Beacon*. But it's new editor was forcing the paper into a tabloid format, the antithesis of what Jack had always fought for.

Every morning, Kara would visit Pa at Twin Oaks. He was now settled into his routine and happy as ever. His dementia was also "on hold" and he seemed to be clearer in his memories. Still, it was unsettling to think that he would live out what was left of his days among a revolving door of strangers. Already one of his pals had passed. Thank goodness for Daniel, who was a steadying presence in Pa's life. Still, it wasn't the way Kara wanted things to be.

And while Kara and Joe were essentially engaged, she wasn't yet ready for a wedding. Another October passed. There was a remembrance mass at Jimmy's old parish on the two-year anniversary of his death. On the same day, the publisher of the *Beacon* told staff and freelancers that he was putting the paper up for sale. The tabloid format wasn't working. It even alienated the *Beacon's* few remaining loyal readers.

Halloween came. Children, costumed as superheroes and fairy princesses, scampered through falling leaves, trick-or-treating from house to house. Kara and Mrs. Mullins took turns manning the front door, handing out Snickers and Reese's candy bars. But among the Halloweeners was a tall, gawky bespectacled man. He carried a briefcase and the thin strands of hair he had carefully arranged across his head were blowing wildly in the wind as he made his way up the front steps of the Mullins residence. It was Dennis Gregson.

"Kara? I'm sorry it took me so long. Nancy's estate was quite complicated."

He took her off guard. In truth, Kara had placed any thoughts of Nancy Harding's estate on the back burner of her mind. It was a troubling subject. That will had caused two murders. Nancy's selfishness had also, indirectly, brought about Biff Daniels' demise. Though Jack sabotaged the brakes on Biff's motorcycle, had Nancy not left her children for her buff costar, the teenaged Jack would likely not have lashed. So in Kara's mind, no amount of money was worth all the heartache Nancy's estate had already caused.

"It's been a trying time for everyone, Dennis. And I'm sure you had your share of problems as a result of that will."

"Well, Nancy, your birth mother, had many investments. And when Biff died, she inherited *his* money as well. Both of them, when they began making those silly beach movies, well, someone gave them good advice. They cleverly asked for points in every picture."

"I don't understand."

"She and Biff owned a piece of the profits from their films. And those stupid films were distributed all over the globe. Translated into fifty languages."

"Are you saying that was how she paid her bills at Twin Oaks?"

"I'm saying she left a fortune. I have been settling her debts, and now I can distribute what is left. Of course, it will be divided by thirds. Ricky Wexner, yourself and the Mullins as surrogates for their son. With Jack in prison for life without parole, his cut is automatically forfeited."

Kara thought of the irony of it all. Jack, who wanted the money only to please Sue, was left with nothing. No money. No freedom. A life behind bars. "I'm glad the Mullins will get something."

"Don't you want to know what you inherit?"

"Well I know Jack already took Nancy's black sedan. It nearly pushed me off the road."

"He stole that car. And it was intended for you."

Kara winced. "I don't want it. Donate it to charity."

"I thought you'd want to do that."

"So we're settled now."

"Not really. There's the rest of your inheritance."

"Oh …" Kara figured if she got a few thousand dollars to help her pay first and last month's rent on her own place, she'd be happy.

"It totals forty-nine."

"Oh?" She perked up. "Forty-nine thousand. I can get a nice apartment for that."

"No, Kara. Forty-nine million …. Forty-nine million six hundred fifty-two thousand dollars to be exact."

Kara mentally replayed what Dennis had just said. "Dennis, would you repeat that figure?" And he did … then reiterated that the Mullins and Ricky Wexner would be inheriting the same amount.

Kara sat down as Dennis unlocked his briefcase and took out some papers for her to sign. There was also an identical set of papers for the Mullins to sign, which left the elderly couple so shocked and bewildered that they were sure they heard Dennis incorrectly … until he had to point out the total amount in print so they'd be able to process their new largesse.

"Holy Mother of God," was all Mrs. Mullins could say. While Mr. Mullins asked if it would be alright if he ordered himself a new car with the money.

"You can buy yourself a fleet of cars if you like," Dennis smiled.

Chapter Fifty-six

The Mullins used their inheritance to honor their son. They established college scholarships, "full freight," meaning room and board, for ten Nelligan students every year. The criteria was simple. The scholarship winners were not judged on their academic excellence, but on their character. Those who exhibited kindness and a readiness to help others were singled out by teachers and other students as worthy of winning "a Mullins" as it was called. They also gave a million dollar check to Father Jim's former parish to help with repairs and upkeep.

Unfortunately, Ricky Wexner took his cut of the estate and spent it as soon as he left the rehabilitation facility, getting high with his so-called "friends."

Kara knew immediately what she wanted to do with the money. She bought a large acreage in the Country Estates region, on a pond, and asked Joe if he would oversee construction of "their" dream home.

The house included a wheel chair accessible wing for Pa if he decided to live there, as well as a private area for a nurse. The rest of the home was spacious and full of light. A huge hearth sat in the main room and the upstairs bedrooms all had skylights that offered an amazing night view of the stars. In the kitchen, Kara insisted it overlook the pond.

On the far end of the property, Kara wanted a barn for horses. She always wanted to own a horse. And attached to the barn would be a rescue shelter for feral cats and stray dogs. She named it "The Paw Palace."

The following October, on a brilliantly sunny day decorated with oak and maple leaves scattered on the ground, Kara Fitzgerald and Joe Collins were married at Father Jim's old parish. They honeymooned in their new home and enjoyed gourmet dinners every night prepared by their new housekeeper, Maria.

And as the *Beacon's* new owner and editor, Kara was anxious to bring the daily newspaper back to its full glory as a reliable news source for the area. There was no concern about growing advertising revenue. But the ads started coming. It seems that many area residents were tired of getting their news online and still enjoyed the daily ritual of having their morning coffee as they perused a real newspaper that got ink on their fingers and stuck to "just the facts."

Pa visited Kara and Jim's place often. Whenever he stayed for a few days, he brought along Daniel, who Kara paid handsomely for helping her father navigate through his final years with dementia.

That August, Kara made Pa a grand"pa" when she gave birth to a boy. She and Joe named their son "James Desmond Collins" after two important men in Kara's life.

And they all lived happily ever after.

The End

About the Author

Marianne Flatley Correri has been writing since the seventh grade. After a long career in TV, film, advertising and public relations, she now enjoys writing books from her home in New Jersey where she lives with her family.